# UNRAVEL

CLUB V - BOOK 1

JESSA JAMES

**GET A FREE BOOK!**

Join my mailing list to be the first to know of new releases, free books, special prices and other author giveaways.

http://freehotcontemporary.com

Unravel: Copyright © 2018 by Jessa James

All Rights Reserved. No part of this book may be reproduced or transmitted in any form or by any means, electrical, digital or mechanical including but not limited to photocopying, recording, scanning or by any type of data storage and retrieval system without express, written permission from the author.

Published by Jessa James
James, Jessa
Unravel

Cover design copyright 2020 by Jessa James, Author
Images/Photo Credit: DepositPhotos: VitalikRadko

Publisher's Note:

This book was written for an adult audience. The book may contain explicit sexual content. Sexual activities included in this book are strictly fantasies intended for adults and any activities or risks taken by fictional characters within the story are neither endorsed nor encouraged by the author or publisher.

This book has been previously published.

## ABOUT UNRAVEL:

*Mr. Vance*

My eyes raked over her. The temporary bartender brought into my office because she'd seen the virgin auction room. I took in her delicious curves and knew I needed to have her. Except, I would never see her again after tonight. But, I always get what I want, I'm the owner of Club V and I will unravel her in ways she's never experienced. I can barely wait to touch and lick every curve of her virgin body.

*Samara*

I assumed the auction room at Club V was just a rumor. Until I walked into the wrong room. I feared being fired but when the guard brought me to Mr. Vance I was instantly a hot mess. He was gorgeous, arrogant, cocky even and I couldn't take my eyes off the very naked woman wearing a diamond collar standing beside him. The look of lust and sex on her face as he played with her and then the way he watched me, teasing. But, I'd never have to see him again after tonight. That is until fate changed everything... God help me!

If cocky men, virgins and angst are your thing read on...

**1**
———

The music from the club throbbed and made its way out onto the street where I stood, pausing to catch my breath before making my way into work. The alleyway stank of stale cigarette smoke and worse, something stinking in one of the dumpsters nearby. I gagged a little and steeled myself as I moved toward the door, not ready to end my break just yet. I couldn't put a finger on why I was feeling the way I did that day, but I was anxious about going into work that night and somewhere in the pit of my stomach it seemed like something was just a little...off.

"You never have to do anything you don't want to," I said to myself, sure that I must look like some kind of a lunatic as I stood outside of the club and tried to think of a reason not to go in. There were far too many reasons that I had to be there. If I ever wanted to finish college I was going to have to keep up things at my job.

It wasn't the sort of work I had always dreamed of doing, but it was paying the bills, keeping food on the table, and whenever my schooling was all done I would be one of the few people I knew who wasn't weighted down under a pile of student loans. The club paid me well for the work I did, which made it all a little easier to deal with — and it was certainly better than the dozen or so waitressing jobs I had picked up through the end of high school and start of college.

And if I was totally honest with myself, I knew that it was all a necessity. My parents couldn't afford to send me to college and if I wanted to continue my education and have a career I was going to have to fund it all myself. If they had been able, I knew my parents would have paid for my schooling, housing, and everything else that came along with college life in a heartbeat, but we just didn't have that kind of lifestyle. My mom had been a secretary at the same law firm since after my younger brother was born. He was only 17 now and she certainly had not been working long enough to work up to any kind of retirement. She joked that she would still be sitting behind the same desk at Keller, Lawson, Waterman, and Keller when she was 75, but deep down I prayed that it would not be the case for her. Money was too tight and she and my dad did everything they could, but I didn't want to see her working into her golden years.

My dad had been in business for himself since he was very young. He was a mechanic and had started off at one of the local garages in town before working his way up and saving enough to buy his own garage and go into business for himself. It was a successful business and he was a great mechanic, doing the kind of work that made people want to come back to him. He had to have been one of the few honest mechanics working in an area already steeped in poverty and his low prices and trustworthy service made him the sort of guy people wanted to give repeat business to.

But even with all of their hard work it would still never be enough. I didn't want to be any part of an added burden to my family so I had decided to take on the tuition and housing on my own. If I could save them from any additional worry and ensure that they could help my brother if he needed it when he started college, I was going to do my part. It had always been like that—working together for the common good for our family. I valued them all so much and cherished the relationships we shared.

I looked at my phone. Suzy had already arrived for her shift sometime during my break and I knew she would be wondering where I was if I took any more time to stand out on the sidewalk contemplating my fate. My god, what was wrong with me this evening? Nothing had changed with work and there was no reason for this hesitation. Not a reason I could put my finger on anyway. There was something in the air and I felt like anything was possible that evening, but I wasn't sure any of it was good.

I pushed the door of the alleyway entrance open and stepped into the area near the back of the bar. A few of the servers were rushing around, dressed in their club issued, all-black attire. The guys had ties in a rich, deep scarlet color that matched the decor around the floor of the club and the girls who waited tables in this area were always instructed to keep their makeup to the same tone. I was just glad that I had the skin tone that worked well with the deep red lipstick I had to wear each night, but upon reflection I had a good idea that we were all hired based on how we would work with the color scheme in the part of the club we would be working in.

There was already a crowd surrounding the bar although it wasn't late yet, our peak time for club members to show up, and I smiled thinking that there might be an extra tip or two in the cards for me tonight.

"Hey Tommy," I said giving a wink and a quick shoulder squeeze to one of our Friday night regulars.

"Samara, baby..." he grinned and turned to pull me toward him, ignoring the fact that I was trying to make my way to the employee dressing rooms. "Sweetheart, don't leave me. You know you're my favorite."

I felt his eyes scouring up and down my body as his hand drifted down to my hip and pulled me suddenly against him. I could feel the start of an erection growing in his pants and while a part of me wondered what it would be like to have Tommy Rollins—investment banker to the upper echelons of New Jersey society—be my first, I just smiled and put a hand on his chest.

"And you're one of mine. Don't ever forget it." I gave him a little grind before turning on my heel and heading off in the direction of the dressing room. I let out an inaudible groan under the heavy beat of the club. It would be great to have someone like Tommy be my first—I knew for a fact that he was good in bed and that women were always clawing to get to the front of the line to be with him in the club. But I also had to keep in mind that I was here as a bartender—the co-head bartender with my best friend and roommate, Suzy, and I wouldn't let the animal attraction I felt to one of the hottest, richest guys in the club jeopardize my job status.

But god, I was aching. Nineteen and still a virgin, I was in the minority among all of my friends, most of whom had given it up when we were in junior high or high school to one of the stupid guys we were surrounded by. Nothing about the thought of losing my virginity to one of these small-town, no future dudes had appealed to me in the least. While it had started off as me making some kind of statement about my standards, now it was just frustrating. I was 19 and I could have sex if I wanted, with anyone I wanted, and there had been so many opportunities. Why hadn't I taken any of them?

"You know why," I said to myself as I moved along

the back wall of the club, heading to find Suzy getting ready for her shift.

I hadn't taken up any of the many offers to deflower me because none of them seemed like they would be a good first. So many casual dates and it wasn't any wonder that none of them had turned into anything. I quickly discovered that a portion of the male population would drop a girl like a hot potato if she wouldn't have sex by the third date. Strangely, there were some that ran for the hills the moment they found out I was a virgin. I had assumed, and was apparently mistaken, that virginity was valued among men—some kind of trophy they collected. It had never occurred to me that some men were put off or intimidated by it.

And so there had been a long string of guys, mostly assholes, who had given me the heave-ho after I told them I was waiting for the perfect time and perfect person.

I pulled back the velvet curtain that shielded the entrance of the employee dressing area from view. It was tucked back in a corner and down a small hallway, housing the lockers for all of the female servers, dancers, and other employees.

"Heya," Suzy called from where she sat in front of one of the vanity mirrors. She was planted on a velvet cushion that matched the same red that covered most of the upholstered surfaces in the club.

"Hi, ready for a long night? Looks like the place is pretty crowded." I took a seat on one of the cushions facing my roommate and watched her as she continued preparing her look for the night.

"Yeah, I think Stew said they were running an ad in one of those flight magazines that caters to...you know, our crowd. Probably a lot of newbies out there tonight. Best to keep our game faces on."

I nodded. I knew what Suzy meant. There were a few hard rules about our jobs here, most important of which was that we were bartenders—nothing more. There was always room for advancement, but that would entail a different sort of contract negotiation with our manager and probably the big wigs who were over him at the club. With new people in the club that night there was a good chance that they wouldn't know that we—the bartenders—weren't on the menu. It was something that could be confusing to people new to the scene, but something we had to remind people from time to time. Even my flirtation with Tommy, while totally above board and the kind of thing expected of me in my role keeping the customers happy, did edge close to a line.

Everyone on the bar and serving staff had to deal with it on occasion. A man or woman who saw us and wanted to do the same things with us that they did with the other people who worked here at Club V. While open sex, partner swapping, and BDSM were all things on the menu at the club, patrons had to understand that the bar staff were not. A giggle had rippled through the small group of new employees at my introductory staff meeting when our manager had said that we weren't 'trained' to do what the other members of the staff were. However, it had always been on the table that a person could move into that line of work at the club if they were interested, but that the two job roles were not to be combined.

I hardly even noticed the sex anymore, now that I was behind the bar almost full-time. When I started off serving there had been more exposure to it as I delivered drinks and small plates to the main floor of the club, which was usually filled with people chatting and enjoying each other's company, but often got a lot heavier than that. More than once I had delivered a drink to a man who insisted on having a sip of a 50 year scotch while a young blonde woman bounced up and down on his cock wildly. Sex was allowed on the main floor, as it was allowed anywhere in the club, but mostly occurred in the small alcoves that surrounded the large room on the ground floor. The large bar presided over the main room and saw a lot of business, but very often people in the alcoves or down the large hall would order something that had to be delivered to them.

In those early days I saw a lot more than I did now and I no longer noticed the moaning that emanated from the alcoves. The DJ usually kept the music going loud enough to drown that out anyway, or played something that the moans complemented. There was no denying the overtly sensual environment of my workplace. Every inch of the 5,000 square foot club throbbed with a sexual beat and the smell of ylang ylang, sandalwood, and patchouli stirred up the lust of all who entered the place, while simultaneously attempting to mask the unmistakable aroma of sex and pulsing pheromones. I tried not to think about it so often, but it wasn't odd for me to enter the club and immediately become wet and aroused. That by itself made my current situation that much more difficult to bear.

"How are things going with Kevin?" Suzy asked, pulling me from my thoughts as she looked in the mirror and carefully applied a set of false eyelashes to her left eye. The results were amazing as she leaned back and blinked, taking in her reflection. It was no wonder that Suzy was approached to work here by one of the owners. My good friend and roommate stood about 5 inches taller than me and she looked like she had just walked off the runway at the Victoria's Secret fashion show. Her high, full breasts were a marvel and it made sense why half the men in the club immediately turned their attention toward her stunning figure. Even fully clothed, Suzy was the woman every guy in the club wanted and she was completely out of reach for them.

"Ugh...Kevin. Well, that's over."

When I had left our apartment for work earlier in the day I had been on the phone with Kevin, hashing out an argument we had continued from the night before. In the end it looked like we weren't going to be able to come to any sort of agreement.

Suzy looked my way and gave me a sad frown. Pulling me close, she gave me a hug, careful not to smudge her carefully applied makeup. She had a super thick cat eye look going on tonight and it made her look twice her normally sexy self. She was in school to be a makeup artist so she was always trying out new looks that never failed to impress the clientele at Club V.

"Thanks," I said as I pulled back from the hug. "I'm just going to freshen up a little bit and then I'll be out there to join you."

"See you in a few then," Suzy said as she stood and smoothed out her tight miniskirt and pulled back the curtain to head out to the bar.

I turned and looked at my own reflection. No one else was coming on shift soon so I had the place to myself and could check out my appearance without anyone witnessing it.

My long, wavy blonde hair was down, the way I usually wore it and had a tousled kind of beachy look to it. No wonder Tommy had reached for me. I had to admit it was about as sexy as my hair ever looked and it made me grin. My hazel eyes, flecked with green looked a little mysterious and were just unique enough that I always got compliments on them, especially in the low light of the club. The sconces, bar, and table lighting provided just the right amount of luminescence to make them sparkle brightly. I had been told more than once that they were mesmerizing and I always tried to do my eye makeup in green and gold tones to accentuate this feature.

My high cheek bones, inherited from my grandmother, didn't hurt my overall appearance either. I had no need for contouring as it was already there and I was grateful for that small, genetic mercy. A mole above my upper lip had been an annoyance to me as a child, but now it was the sort of provocative beauty mark that men and women alike complimented me on constantly.

I stood then and frowned. The one thing I would change about myself if I could was my height. At five feet, four inches tall I was one of the shorter women on the bar staff and it made reaching things on the high shelves a job for Suzy instead of me. But my weight was in check and my hips flared to a kind of curve that I knew caught the eye of many people I walked past. My breasts were the show stoppers though. I might have been on the short and smaller side at 125 pounds, but my 38C breasts were something I took a lot of pride in showing off whenever I could. The club allowed Suzy and I to wear our own clothing instead of the standard club issued uniforms and she and I usually chose tight, extremely low cut tanks or scoop-necked t-shirts. It was one of the more comfortable things about our job—we got to be the fun girls at the bar and most of the time it didn't even feel like work.

I smoothed out my own miniskirt and turned to take a look at my backside.

"You've got a fabulous ass," I said to myself with a laugh and turned to make my way back out to the bar, for another night at Club V.

## 2

"Who's ready for another round?" I called across the crowded bar, waving a large bottle of reposado tequila toward the patrons with a wink. I received a few 'whoop's' and nods and after I had poured another 12 shots I returned with a $50 bill between my now sweating breasts, placed there ever so generously by Tommy along with his business card, to stand beside Suzy who was adding drinks to a tab.

"Seriously, the ad must have worked. I cannot believe how many new faces I'm seeing here tonight."

Suzy was right. The place was buzzing with the energy of new visitors to the club and I hoped it meant that plenty of them would be signing up for membership. I knew that once a lot of these people got a taste of what the club had to offer they would have a hard time not returning to scratch the itch it inevitably infected them with.

"You're doing a great job," I said, bumping her with my hip. "Really, the place hasn't been like this in a long time and I think Stew is going to noticed we've stepped up to the plate."

"Look who's talking," Suzy said as she grinned and looked down at the $50 bill I pulled out of my cleavage. "Girl, they love you here. Don't you ever forget it. They couldn't ask for a better bartender than you. You're going places."

I smiled, happy that the strange feeling in my stomach from earlier in the night had left me. I was still uncertain where it had all been coming from. Maybe it was nothing more than my run in with Kevin on the phone that had made me feel funny about coming into work tonight. Either way, I put the thoughts aside and focused on what was in front of me. Suzy was right—I was making tips hand over fist and at this rate I would be able to pay down double on my loans this month. I knew how lucky I was to have this job and there was nothing in the world that was going to lure me away from the club.

"Ladies!" My brief reverie was over as our manager, Stew, made his way through the crowd and behind the bar. Stew was a massive guy at 6'7' and 290 pounds. A former linebacker, he was now in charge of all the sales here at the club.

He looked around and motioned a hand down the length of the bar. "You two are amazing. Thank you so much for taking on the extra burden of all the new patrons. I don't think the owners knew just how well it was going to pay off when they placed that ad, but here we are and it looks like it's going to be amazing."

"Happy to see it," I said with a genuine smile.

"Now that I've sufficiently oiled the cogs, I do have a favor to ask you specifically, Samara."

I raised an eyebrow. "Okay?"

"I know tomorrow is your day off, but—"

"Do you need me to come in? That's no problem." I blurted the words out. I was always happy to pick up an extra shift.

Stew shook his head. "Well, not exactly. I'm going to bump Lori up to help out Suzy tomorrow night, but I was wondering if you would be able to go to the New York location tomorrow night? They have a big event and combined with the added traffic because of that ad campaign, they need as many hands on deck as they can get. You'll be paid time and a half."

My eyes went wide. I had never worked at the New York location of Club V before. I hadn't ever stepped a foot inside the place, but I knew about it by reputation. And the reputation was that they pulled in the real high rollers. Sure, here in New Jersey we saw quite a bit of money coming through the doors thanks to the people who lived in bedroom communities out here and worked high paying jobs in the city, as well as the folks who had jobs in the gambling industry or who were making their money that way.

But New York City! Bright lights, big city...and

people with crazy, insatiable sexual appetites. I guess I just needed to hope that they liked their drinks bottomless as well.

"Absolutely. No problem, Stew. I didn't have anything on my schedule anyway." I gave Suzy a glance, thinking of our earlier conversation regarding my now defunct relationship with Kevin.

"Great! I'll make the call and let them know you'll be there. Shift starts at 7:00 pm, maybe show up a little earlier so that they can show you the lay of the land. Oh, and you'll need to grab one of the Club V button down blouses. They're a little more strict about the look the bartenders have going on at that location."

I nodded excitedly and kept myself from rushing Stew with a hug. He talked to us a little more about some upcoming events at the club and then disappeared back into his office.

Suzy turned to look at me, her eyes wide. "You're going to work at NYC!"

"Just for a night..."

"Yeah, but you never know what it could turn into. And my god, you know how much money they see at that location...well, I mean, we don't really know, but you know it is like major. That $50 Tommy slid between your boobs? Yeah, try something closer to $1000 in New York. Have you ever even seen a $1000 bill?" Suzy leaned against the wall and let out a breathless sigh.

"I doubt anyone is going to slide $1000 between my boobs."

Suzy shook her head. "You're right, that's not how they roll up there." She leaned in close to whisper with a giggle. "They'll try to slide it in your pussy!"

I swatted at her and glared momentarily before going to fill another glass of wine. When I returned she was still laughing.

"But seriously, Samara, you know you're going to have to watch it up there. I've never been, but I've heard that they do things a little differently around that place. You know what they say…about that room."

Anyone unfamiliar with the reputation of Club V wouldn't know what 'room' Suzy was talking about, but having worked at the New Jersey location for a year now I was well aware of the rumors that surrounded the club.

People said it was an auction room where men could come to buy women for their own pleasure and purposes. It was all rumored, of course, and no one that either Suzy or I knew had ever seen one of the rooms. Club V had a nationwide presence and they were growing by the year. If the rumors were true, Club V had an auction room at all of their major locations—New York, Los Angeles, Las Vegas, Chicago, and Dallas. What happened in those auction rooms a person could only dream about because as far as I knew, no living breathing person that I had ever met, with any connection to the club, had ever stepped foot inside one.

"You know, that could all be some kind of an urban legend. You know how those kinds of stories get started. Probably a waitress at one of the places saw something happening in one of the private rooms she didn't understand, she told a friend and there you go. It's a game of telephone and no one knows where it started."

Suzy shrugged and handed one of the bar patrons a receipt to sign. "All I'm saying is…" she moved closer to me to speak in a hushed tone. "You need to keep your head high and stay strong at a place like that. You know why I'm here? I know I can trust Stew. I wouldn't be here if we didn't have the kind of manager I knew I could put my complete trust in. While I have faith in the Club V brand—you know as well as I do how well they vet their members—NYC is the biggest club they have and I've heard stories about what some of the people show up there wanting. Sure, there's BDSM going on around here but I'd say it's pretty light. New York has the most elite, exclusive kind of access. They cater to their patrons' every whim. You just need to make sure you don't catch anyone's eye or become a whim."

I rolled my eyes. "Look, I'll be wearing the uniform. And like you said—the place is super elite and exclusive. If the guys here know that we aren't to be bothered, I am certain that the members at that location are aware of the rule as well."

Suzy finally nodded. "I really am happy for you, Samara. I know that working time and a half at NYC will probably be close to two weeks of your regular work here and I know you can use that cash. Honestly, I'm probably a little jealous." She said the last bit with a grin. "And feel free to give my number to any of the eligible ones you run into. If they're members at the NYC location then there aren't any stipulations about me dating them."

I nodded and smiled at my best friend. "That's right, your own personal matchmaker right here. What in the world would you do without me?"

She waved her hand nonchalantly. "Keep dating losers, clearly."

"You've had better luck than I have," I said with a hint of bitterness in my voice. It would have been really great to have any of the short lived relationships I had been involved in since I first started college turn out to be more than just passing time, but I had almost resigned myself to no longer worrying about getting dates. There would always be men, that much I knew. I would be doing myself a favor if I spent time focusing on school and work.

"True," Suzy agreed. She was looking out over the crowd as it began to thin.

Later in the evening people moved on to the alcoves or the private areas. The private rooms filled up quickly, the first of which were always the voyeur rooms with a glass panel in the voyeur hall. I had trekked down that hall several times but it never failed to shock and titillate when I realized I was surrounded on all sides by naked bodies, writhing in pleasure.

From our station at the main bar we could look out across the expanse of the large main room and see the pool where a few people were in skimpy bathing suits or nothing at all. It was all quite spectacle this time of night, but at the bar things began to quiet. There would still be a few people there for drinks, those who had already partaken of whatever they were going to do at the club that night, or those who treated the bar like what it was—a place where they could air their troubles to a kind listening ear. And in the case of me, Suzy, and everyone else tending at Club V, our patrons got an eyeful to carry home with them every evening.

"I wouldn't hate to have a wealthy guy though, you know, like one of the sort we see around here," Suzy mused.

I surveyed the room. "You really think you want a guy who would show up here?"

She shrugged as she started wiping down an area behind the bar.

"Of course not here, specifically, since it isn't allowed. But yeah, I think I wouldn't mind a guy from one of the other clubs. Just to get treated well for a little while."

I thought carefully about what I was going to say

next. No one was around to hear me and I would never say anything in front of a patron, but I had reservations about some of these guys.

"You don't mind...you know, what they're into? Some of them can get a little scary."

"I know what you mean. There are a few, really vanilla guys, around here though. I'm sure NYC has some folks who are just there to fuck or watch other people. Not everyone is into butt plugs and ball gags, but I'm not judging your taste, Samara." She elbowed me with a laugh.

I just smiled and brushed her off. "Yeah, I really don't think that's my style."

Suzy gave me a half smile. "You'll never know until you try. Have you given that much thought?"

"Butt plugs and ball gags?"

Suzy rolled her eyes. "No, finally handing in that v-card of yours. I don't ever want to put any pressure on you and I know you have your reasons, but I think it might be a good thing for you to just let go a little. It doesn't have to be perfect the first time. I'd challenge you to find many people who would describe their first time as perfect. It's usually clumsy and messy and awkward."

I cleared away a few glasses and stacked them in a drainer where they would later be taken to the back to be washed.

"You make love sound like so much fun, Suzy.

Really, anyone would be champing at the bit to get at something like that."

She held a finger in the air. "Ah, see! That's where you're confused. You're talking about love and I'm talking about some good, old-fashioned fucking. Just letting loose and going after it with a guy. Find one a little older, make sure he knows what he's doing. They say making sure they can dance is a good indicator. Just find yourself one and go for it." Suzy reached out and rubbed my arm. "You've got the body of a goddess! There are dozens of guys here every night who would die to get into bed with you. And if they knew you were a virgin...holy shit, Samara. Men worship women in that situation."

I frowned at her. She absolutely knew that wasn't the kind of response I had encountered when guys I dated found out I had never had sex.

"Umm, what? No way. Every guy I've dated hasn't been into that. Or wanted to push me so far, so fast, that I had to get away."

"That is because you are dating boys, baby. It's time you found yourself a man to date. I'm serious. You need to find yourself a full-grown gentleman who knows what's up. Keep your eyes peeled in NYC. Those executive types are always crowding those places. You need to find one to help you out and then never let that guy go."

# 3

The train ride into the city the next evening was long and unfamiliar. I could have driven but that would have just been a nightmare. I had found a subway map on my phone and was referring to it every once in a while to make sure I didn't miss my stop. Unwilling to be mistaken for a tourist, I held my head high and tried to give off an air of knowing what I was doing, even though I was a little afraid to be traveling to the city on my own. It wasn't something I did much of and though I felt very confident in my own abilities, I couldn't let my guard slip and discount the kind of crime that women sometimes experienced on public transit.

It was a rude reminder a few stops down the line, when an older man got on the train and stood in front of my seat, his crotch almost in my face. I got up and moved down the train only to find him close at my heels. Uncertain of his intentions—whether pervy or just downright criminal—I stood next to another woman and watched the man as he stopped and stared at me, a wide, gold-toothed grin spreading across his face.

It had been a mistake to get on the train already dressed for work. Fishnets, heels, and a miniskirt spelled one thing to people on the train and I just hoped that I looked high end if they were going to make their assumptions. For the duration of the ride I ignored the unwanted attention and finally reached my stop, hopping up and rushing out the doors, along the platform, and up the steps to the street level.

Club V was only a few blocks away from the subway stop and I made it there in almost no time without any further issues from people I met on the street. This Club V, much like the one back at home, was understated from the outside. It seemed to be more of an issue of discretion here though, as many of their clients were actually elite members of society. Sure, back home we had our own and often entertained men that were known to be part of mob families, but here they entertained actors, diplomats, members of the news media, and politicians who were in town making the rounds on various news outlets.

Club V NYC was in what had at one point been a textile factory. It was two stories and each story was slightly exaggerated in height, with the tall windows so common to factories built over a hundred years ago. Most of these windows appeared to be blacked out from the inside to maintain the ambiance Club V was known for, but the beauty of the old building was rather stunning from the outside. Other than the words "CLUB V" on an engraved brass plate near the front door, a person would never know what happened behind these walls. I had a feeling many still didn't, because you couldn't use Google to find out much about this place. I knew because I had tried many times before I took the initial job offer over a year before.

I made my way around the side and pressed a button on the employee entrance.

"Yes?" A voice rang out over an intercom.

"Umm…hi. I'm Samara, Samara Tanza. From the New Jersey location. I'm here to bartend for the evening."

There was a pause and for a moment I wondered if I was going to be turned away and dreaded the long train ride back home.

"Right, right. I'll buzz you in."

There was a buzz and a click and I was able to open the heavy door that stood between me and the inside of Club V. It was so heavy that it shut behind me quickly and hard, pushing me inside the small foyer. It was total blackness for a moment and I had to give my eyes a second to adjust to the absence of light. After a few seconds it was clear that it wasn't truly dark inside, only dim and especially so in this small area of the club.

A woman in a short, skin-tight red bandage dress appeared as if from nowhere and smiled at me, offering her hand in greeting.

"Samara...it's a delight to meet you. I'm Elle, the director of staffing here. Why don't you follow me. Jake wanted to see you before you were sent to orientation with one of our lead bartenders."

I wasn't sure who Jake was, but assumed that he was the NYC version of Stew and so I followed Elle down the hall to one of the offices.

"Jake is one of our co-owners. He just wanted to do a little run down of a few company policies and let you know what the expectations are here at the NYC location. I'm sure it's all mostly what you've been used to in New Jersey, but there may be a few differences. We pride ourselves on maintaining a very exclusive list of members and do everything we can to preserve their privacy. I think you'll understand what I'm getting at there."

I nodded, then realizing she couldn't see me as I followed her, so I spoke up. "Oh, right. Of course. Yes, we never talk about any of our patrons outside of the club."

"That's great," Elle said. I could hear the smile in her voice. "I'm sure you'll enjoy getting to know Jake. Here's his office."

The office was on the far corner and the door

opened to reveal some of those massively tall windows I had seen from the outside, only these weren't covered and the late evening light filtered into the dim office.

"Jake, this is Samara," Elle said. She smiled and shut the door behind her, leaving me standing there as Jake turned around slowly in his office chair and stood to greet me.

He grinned as he stood there with his hands stuffed in his front pockets, the light gray suit he wore was well-tailored and fit him perfectly. He was a tall, stunning picture of a man with jet black hair, full lips, olive skin and eyes that hovered somewhere between blue and gray.

I was silent and realized I had been staring, and that he had been also. Unsure of who was expected to speak first, I finally spoke up.

"Hi...Jake."

He nodded. "I like to see all the new people we bring on board. Just to get an idea of who is new on the floor and who might need some assistance." He moved around his desk and came forward to greet me, reaching out a hand to shake mine. "Samara? Lovely name." His words were like butter. I was sure but it sounded like he had the slightest hint of an accent and that made this already incredible looking hunk of a man even more attractive.

"Thank you," I said, trying to play it as cool as I could. If everyone around this place looked half as good as Jake did, it was going to be a long, but fun night full of eye candy.

"I hope you'll enjoy your time here. And not that I am looking to poach someone from one of our other locations, but you can be certain that someone of your calibre is always welcome here at Club V NYC. I've heard what a great bartender you've been in Jersey and you come highly recommended."

I felt my face flush. "Well, Stew is really kind. I've enjoyed working at Club V over the past year and couldn't imagine a better place for myself."

Jake rubbed his chin thoughtfully. "What are your long-term goals regarding employment with us?"

No one had ever asked me that question before, other than Stew when he promoted me to bartender after I had been serving for a few months.

"I've really enjoyed bartending. To be honest with you it's the thing that I'm doing to pay for my college tuition. It's been great for that. The tips are wonderful and I've been able to pay for everything myself so far, without any help from my parents."

Something seemed to flash across Jake's face. "How old are you?"

"Nineteen," I answered, not missing a beat.

"Wow...I guess I just assumed you were a little older than that. Oh well, still legal."

The phrase jarred me and I was sure my eyes went wide.

"I mean...legal to bartend in both New Jersey and

New York," he added with a laugh. "But seriously, did you ever want to move beyond that here?"

It was dawning on me what Jake, one of the co-owners of Club V, was asking me. This guy not only owned this club, he was part owner in all the clubs across the United States and now there was one in every state.

Calm yourself, Samara. He asks every single woman who darkens this door the same question. Now answer him.

"You mean...am I interested in working the floor?"

Working the floor. It was what we called it. It was what the women who did it called it, rather than being too blunt about it. 'I work the floor at Club V' was something you could say in public and sound respectable, when the truth was that working the floor meant that you were paid for sex with one or many men, with varying degrees of BDSM and other acts mixed in.

"That's what I'm asking you, yes."

I would be lying if I said that I hadn't considered working the floor before. I knew the kind of money the girls made and it was so tempting. While they had contracts with the club, they were also allowed to carry on 'professional relationships' with the most elite club members outside of the club, with Club V acting as a sort of intermediary or broker in the dealings. That part was all hush-hush. What went on in the club was private and everyone knew it. No one spoke of it outside of the club. Members paid high prices to keep this out of the news.

What all the employees knew was that it was something skirting several different legal lines and that all it would take was one single bust and the wrong thing on the books and the entire thing would be up in smoke. It was organized prostitution on a massive scale, or at least that was how law enforcement and the government would see it if they ever decided to dive deep enough. My guess had always been that Club V had its hooks deep enough in some big fish and that was what prevented any of the locations from being raided.

But was I interested in doing that sort of work myself? I knew we were allowed to set our own comfort levels. I could have been out there on the floor doing nothing but sitting on laps, a few kisses here and there, maybe a hand job from time to time. But I knew that the women who got into it planning only to go so far rarely maintained their boundaries. It was tempting once you got out there, especially when you were being wined and dined by one of the finest men you had ever laid eyes on. When he was telling you over and over again how much he wanted you. That he wanted to take you back to one of the rooms, spread your legs, and dive head first into your pussy. It made me tingle just thinking about it.

Of course I had considered it. And I might have done it if I wasn't still a virgin. For me that had been the linchpin. I wasn't going to give myself up just for that. The money was good, but it wasn't that good. I didn't need that cash that badly.

I shook my head at Jake. "No, I'm not interested in working the floor right now."

He raised an eyebrow. "Not right now, so perhaps in the future?"

I smiled and lowered my eyes slightly. "There are a few things in my personal life I'd like to get sorted before I consider something like that."

Jake nodded and regarded me thoughtfully, moving closer to me. I breathed in sharply, realizing we were only inches apart. I wasn't sure if it was the effect of the club or if I was truly attracted to this man or some combination of the two. He reached out a hand and brushed my hair away from my face.

"Well, keep it in mind if you are ever interested. As far as I'm concerned, there is a standing offer here for you."

"I appreciate that." His hand rested lightly on my shoulder and I could feel my heart racing.

"There's only one thing," he said, frowning and looking down at my blouse. "Your buttons. Do you mind?"

Oh god, had I forgotten to button one of the buttons on my shirt? Was that why I had been getting all the attention on the train? Maybe I had been putting on a peep show for all the riders.

"N-no..." I stammered.

Deftly, Jake unbuttoned two of the buttons on my

blouse, opening it up to reveal an ample amount of cleavage and a hint of the scarlet lace of my bra. Then he removed his hand and backed away politely.

"Club V NYC standards—top four buttons must be unbuttoned. You can head back down the hall and to your right. Celeste will be there to show you around the bar and get you settled."

I left Jake's office stunned. I wasn't sure what I had thought was going to happen, but him unbuttoning my blouse hadn't been it. I didn't think there had been anything truly sexual or inappropriate about it. Honestly, brushing my hair back away from my face was probably worse than the unbuttoning itself. The guy had given me no indication he was attracted to me. The more I thought about it as I walked back down the dimly lit hallway, the more I started to believe that this was probably the line that every girl who walked through the doors of this club to work was fed. Of course they would rather have a young woman on the floor rather than behind the bar.

And my age. That was the kicker. I looked older, so I would not have pulled in the crowd that are looking for the younger ones, but knowing that I was only 19 would really do it for some of these guys. Plus the virgin thing...I made a mental note to keep that to myself. Suzy knew, but Suzy was my best friend and she was back home. There was no need for anyone at this particular establishment to know that small detail about my personal life.

The bar was right where Jake said it would be and I found Celeste standing there looking over an inventory sheet.

"Hi, Celeste?"

She looked up from her clipboard and appeared only slightly annoyed to have been interrupted. I was quickly able to verify that 4 buttons unbuttoned was indeed the Club V NYC standard.

"You must be Samara. Welcome to my bar." She waved her hand in a sweeping motion. "It is my bar. You'll need to remember that. I know you're up to your own standard back home and I'm sure that's a high one and that's fine. But keep in mind that this is my place, I rule the roost, and while I'm happy to help you out at first, you are here to assist me. It's not the other way around."

I nodded. "Got it."

She gave me a once over. "I see you've met with Jake and he's apprised you of our button policy." She rolled her eyes. "He's harmless for the most part. I'm starting to wonder if it's an inside joke between him and the other owners. Anyway, as long as you aren't ready to run right out of the place and file a sexual harassment law suit, I'm going to assume you're ready to start?"

"Yup, ready to go."

Celeste put the clipboard down. She had a short and serious looking bob and I could tell that everything about this woman was no nonsense.

"So, our setup is pretty standard. I don't think you'll have any trouble behind the bar. We get really busy on Saturday nights and with the ad campaign we're expecting about twice the usual number. I'm not entirely sure that they thought this all the way through, but we're going to have to manage."

Celeste sounded exasperated. "Along with all of this, we've also had a few of our girls move up to floor work here on the main floor as well as upstairs. Do you work the second floor at your club?"

I shook my head. "Not anymore. I used to work it a little off and on when I first started."

"Same sort of setup here, if you do end up going up there. Main open air lounge, a few private spaces, and the sky bar."

The sky bar was one of the few things that drew attention to Club V. I wasn't sure how it would be set up at this location with the kind of architecture the building had going on, but back home the sky bar was a bar that opened up onto a balcony. Plenty of people came to the front door requesting admittance, thinking they could just pop up and have a drink. It seemed to be good advertising and members were far enough away from street level that they were still able to maintain some privacy.

"Overall we have the same basic setup across our various locations, only New York is the biggest. You'll find it may be a little wilder here than you are used to and I don't know if you've been told to be on your guard, but you should. I wouldn't say people here are aggressive, but sometimes they get into a state and aren't paying attention to who is bar staff and who is working the floor, although it should be pretty clear."

I knew what she meant by that. There were floor workers back home, but it wasn't the bulk of the business. It would be too risky to make Club V what boiled down to a brothel. Most people met there for sex. It was more about being in the open with it and finding people who wanted to engage in the same activity as you did. The floor workers were just a perk and part of what kept the place entertaining.

A crowd of businessmen approached the bar then and Celeste's entire demeanor changed. "Gentlemen! What can we get you guys this evening?" Her smile was coy and she gave one of the guys a wink as they all sidled up to the bar. Taking their orders we both began mixing drinks and she turned to me to speak softly.

"You're going to do fine. This place is bigger, the people are more important, but you're here to do the same thing." She looked out over the crowd. "But brace yourself. I think it's going to be a bumpy night."

———

"Cece? We're out of vermouth." One of the bartenders from the other end of the bar called out and it took me a minute to realize he was speaking to Celeste. It had been a very busy night with lots of martini orders and now at midnight it looked like we were out of a crucial component.

"Check the stock room," she replied, trying to keep a smiling face for the patrons in front of her. She was a wiz at the bar and it was no wonder that the men liked to get as close to her as they could. She had the sort of sassy wit that challenged them in conversation, but she was completely out of reach. I found out over the course of the evening that Celeste was happily married to her wife and they had two beautiful children.

"Nope, that's where I got this bottle." The bartender held up and waved around an empty vermouth bottle. "It was the last one."

"Goddammit," Celeste cursed under her breath. "Make sure we order more on Monday. Samara..." she turned to me and narrowed her eyes. "I think I know where we have some extra stock, but it'll be in one of the storage rooms on the second floor. I would call up there and have one of them run it down, but they never answer the phone at the sky bar. Go back to the storage area, take the freight elevator up to the second floor, and it'll deposit you in a hallway. Go right and then left and then right again and there will be a door on your left. Check there for the vermouth. And if there isn't any there just go steal a bottle or two from the sky bar."

"Got it," I said as I squeezed past the rest of the bar staff and headed back to the storage area. The freight elevator was easy enough to find and fired up when I pressed the buttons. It let me out just where Celeste said it would, but by the time the thing reached the landing I had already forgotten the exact directions that Celeste had given me. There was a right and then a left and a door on the left?

I made my way down the hall, turned left, headed down that hallway and instead of coming to any doors I came to a hall on the right and one on the left. Ahead of me I could keep going and I would be on the main part of the second floor. I took a left down the hall, away from the pulsing beats the DJ was churning out, and eventually came to a door. It wasn't on the left though, which confused me, but I opened it and stepped into darkness. It sure looked like a supply room.

I felt along the wall for a light switch, but found nothing. I had my phone in my pocket which I could use as a flashlight if I needed to, but I felt out in front of me to see what exactly I was facing.

My hands touched velvet and went right through the curtain. Suddenly I realized that wherever I was, it was much more spacious than a supply room. When I pushed past the curtain and into a dimly lit area, I could tell that I had definitely taken a wrong turn, but I was too shocked by what I saw to turn around and run.

# 4

*P*art of me wondered what the fuck I was looking at, while another part knew exactly what it was.

At the back of this large room was a stage and on this stage stood five completely naked women, each of whom were collared. There was an auctioneer taking bids on one of the women in the middle of the stage. It all looked very civilized as I saw the gentlemen in the room seated in round booths, some on their own, some with other women, some with what I assumed were business associated.

"This is Clara," the auctioneer read from a leather-bound journal on a podium. "She is 22, a senior at NYU, and has studied ballet for the past 17 years. Turn around for us please, Clara."

I watched as Clara did what she was told, totally mesmerized and aghast at what I was seeing and hearing. They truly were auctioning off women here on the second floor of Club V.

"Clara, like all of our lovely young ladies here this evening, meets all the standard requirements. She is a virgin and as you can tell by the emerald collar, she is willing to engage in sex, a little bondage, and...anal? Do you do anal, Clara?"

Clara turned and smiled coyly at the auctioneer and the crowd and nodded.

"Ah, very good. Why don't you bend over for our bidders."

I watched, transfixed as Clara bent over and spread her cheeks, showing the potential bidders in the audience her ass and pussy. I could hardly believe what I was seeing. I wanted to run, to get out of the room without anyone noticing me, but there was something about it that was so...shocking and scintillating, I almost wanted to see things through to the end.

"Very nice, Clara. You can turn back around now. You'll see Clara has smaller breasts, 30A. She watches her figure for ballet and there's a note here that the bondage must be performed pretty carefully so as not to leave bruises because she has a performance coming up in less than a month." The auctioneer looked out into the crowd. "That means you'd better stay away from this one, Mr. Delaney."

A few members of the crowd of bidders laughed at this and then the auctioneer began asking for bids.

At that point I had had enough. I could not believe

what I was seeing, that all the rumors were true, and that they were auctioning off virgins up here on the second level of Club V. I needed to get out of there and fast before someone noticed me standing there watching the borderline illegal proceedings.

I turned and ran smack dab into a brick wall I didn't remember being there before and then realized it wasn't a brick wall, but one of the largest men I had ever seen and in the low light I could read that his name tag said "Carl."

"How did you get in here?" he whispered gruffly as he grabbed me by the elbow and steered me back out past the velvet curtain, through the door and out into the hallway.

"I was looking for—"

"Did you find what you were looking for? What do you think you're doing nosing around up here? You know you aren't supposed to be in this part of the club. I don't know who the fuck you think you are, but I'm taking you down to Vance's office right now."

My heart raced as the bouncer led me back down the hall and to a different elevator, one that took us down to the hallway that housed the offices. Carl wasn't taking any of my explanation.

"You can talk to Vance about it. You know you aren't supposed to be up there. It's a private area. You'll lose your job over this."

Furious and almost in tears, I crossed my arms across my chest and realized I must look like a sullen child, but I wasn't going to take this treatment from a bouncer. I would explain myself to this Vance guy or Jake, if I could locate him. I'd get Celeste to come in and back me up. I had only been looking for vermouth!

The door to one of the offices stood slightly ajar and Carl knocked on it before leading me inside.

"Mr. Vance, this one was in the auction room."

"Oh really?" The man looked up from the work on his desk, somewhat amused at the sight of me next to massive Carl. "I wonder how the little mouse managed to make her way in there. Were you trying to crawl up on the auction block yourself?"

"I can explain—" I started to say but was cut off.

"I'm sure you can. Carl, thanks for bringing her down. You can head back up in case there are any other infiltrators trying to make their way into the auction."

"Yes sir," Carl said as he turned and left me there in the office with Vance.

"Come in, have a seat. We'll chat."

I followed his instructions, really wanting to do what I could to keep my job. It was clearly going to take a moment to explain, but I knew that once I had Celeste come in to back me up everything would be fine.

I took a seat across from him and now, closer, I could see what a handsome figure this man, who I assumed must be a manager or one of the other owners, really was. He had dark hair and a little stubble on his chin. Just enough to make him look sexy and sort of disheveled. His eyes were a striking deep blue and the rest of him looked like he was a Greek statue that had come to life. At least one with the clothes on. Fuck he was hot!

He caught me staring at him and smiled. "What's your name?"

"Samara Tanza."

"And what are you doing here tonight, Samara Tanza? God, that name just rolls right off the tongue."

I crossed my arms and tried to remain as composed as possible. "I'm here bartending. I'm from the New Jersey location and I was brought in as backup for your bartending staff."

He nodded his head. "Very good. What do you think of the New York club? How does it stack up to Jersey?" He seemed to be trying to put on a Jersey accent and it didn't impress me at all. In fact, it was one of my least favorite things in the world whenever I felt like someone was joking about or criticizing the place that I called home. It was hard enough to overcome the kind of anti-Jersey sentiment that you often found in New York, but seriously to have this guy throwing it in my face was too much.

"Honestly? I prefer Jersey."

He laughed. "Jersey's a great place. I happen to like it a lot myself. I have some family there. So, you want to tell me how you managed to find your way into our most exclusive, private event?"

I shrugged. "It was an accident. We ran out of vermouth and Celeste sent me up to the second floor supply room to find some. I took a wrong turn...probably several wrong turns, and ended up in there."

"And what did you see?"

I let out a long exhale. "I saw a lot. A lot more than I wanted to see."

"Yes, but..." he paused and gave me a long look. "Do you understand what you saw in there?"

When did this guy think I was born? Yesterday? How could a person witness that and not understand?

"I saw a girl named Clara selling her virginity to the highest bidder," I said, my tone clearly indicating what I thought about the way he was questioning me.

Mr. Vance nodded. It was sinking in that I hadn't just arrived on planet earth and knew a little about the world and what was going on.

"Ah yes, Clara. I interviewed her. Sweet girl, she's going to go places." He looked at me with a devilish grin. "Happen to see who got her?"

"I didn't stick around to find out," I answered curtly.

"Probably the prince. He loves his ballerinas. Typically we don't let our bidders return more than a few times each year, but he is so consistent and doesn't mind paying our prices, so how I can say no?" He said as his long think finger lightly tapped his lips as if he was contemplating his own question.

My jaw was hanging wide open and I closed it, not wanting to give away exactly what I thought about this whole arrangement. I believed that women had the right to do whatever they wanted with their bodies, but I had a difficult time believing that any woman would give up her virginity to a total stranger. Except for in this case there was a shit ton of money involved and I knew how tempting something like that could be. Hadn't I been there myself? I certainly wouldn't have walked through the doors of Club V for the first time if it hadn't been for Suzy encouraging me and the fact that I was so desperate for a paycheck.

"Do you have any questions, Samara?" He asked as he steepled his fingers under his chin hold my stare.

"About what?"

"About how we operate, what we're doing here, or how it all works upstairs. And by the way, I'm Neil. You can call me that if you like."

I chewed my lip silently and then spoke. "I have a hard time believing that any young woman would truly want to give herself over to a man like that unless there was a lot of money involved. It feels like coercion."

"I can understand why you might think that," he replied. "The truth is that all of the bidders are thoroughly vetted and so are the women who present themselves for the auction block. No one is being coerced. Everyone is there because they want to be. And I would like to think that everyone leaves the room pleased. Hopefully they're pleased more a little later on." Neil grinned slyly.

"I know there are things that drive people to make those kinds of decisions, it was just…something else to see it so up close and personal. I don't know what I expected, but it wasn't that."

Neil nodded. "Then I would advise you to forget everything you saw. Pretend it never happened. Pretend you never left the bar tonight. I'll get someone to fetch the vermouth for you and you can tell Celeste you were with me. That should keep you out of trouble…well, most of the trouble you could get into with her. I have to be honest with you, Celeste runs her own show around here." He laughed. "Seriously though, forget what you saw. Unless…"

"Unless what?" I frowned.

He lowered his tone and I could swear that his already sexy voice got even huskier. "Unless you liked what you saw."

"Ha! As if." I retorted.

Almost on cue, and completely out of nowhere, a woman walked through the door. And just like the women upstairs on the auction block, she was stark naked except for a collar. Hers was diamond, whereas Clara's had been emerald. But the collar was hardly the thing that would have caught someone's attention. As she entered Neil's office carrying a tray with a drink on it, her breasts bounced, the dark pink tips pointing out and up and completely at attention. She was perfection and her smooth skin was completely hairless. Her lips the same deep dark red that covered most of the surfaces of Club V, she had very little makeup on and her long blond hair was pulled back into a tight ponytail.

"Mr. Vance," she said as she approached his desk and set the drink down.

"Thank you, dear. Samara, this is Asia. She works the second floor and on occasion she likes to bring me a drink. When I tell her to." Neil smacked Asia on the ass and she giggled, then bit her lip as if thinking better of it.

I nodded politely toward Asia, but kept my eyes trained on Neil. The woman was incredibly attractive and it was difficult not to stare at her nude form, but I didn't want Neil to think he had any kind of control over me.

"Back to our discussion—are you sure you didn't like a little of what you saw, Samara? Are you sure none of it was interesting to you in the least?"

I shook my head feeling the wetness of my panties. I wasn't going to admit that for a brief moment while I watched Clara presenting herself before those bidders that I had considered what it would feel like if I were up there, spreading my legs in front of the men and women who were watching. What would it be like to be so on display, listening to people bid and fight over who got to have me for the first time?

"No, not at all," I answered bluntly.

Neil narrowed his eyes and took a sip from his glass. Then as he kept his eyes on mine, he reached over and slid a finger between the lips of Asia's pussy. I fought to keep my face from showing any shock, but had to grip the arms of the chair to keep myself from falling out of it.

He stroked her pussy and I couldn't help my eyes darting over to see that she was already very wet, his finger coated in her slickness. Her eyes were closed and she was pinching both of her nipples as he flicked her clit rhythmically.

I blinked and looked back at Neil.

He smiled at me and raised an eyebrow. "You aren't wondering at all about what's happening to Clara right now? How well she is being fucked by someone who knows how to do it? Can you imagine—a woman's first time being with someone who knows exactly what to do to please her? So many rarely have that opportunity. Seriously, it's got to be an amazing feeling to have someone take their time with you, bring you to the edge over and over again and then finally let you careen over the side...right as he plunges inside you."

I cleared my throat. Asia was moaning audibly now and I was trying not to wriggle around in my chair. I was wet and I knew the feeling had been growing from the moment I saw the girls on the stage upstairs. Now as I watched this exquisitely gorgeous man finger fuck one of the most beautiful women I'd ever laid eyes on, I could barely keep myself from reaching down and...

"Are you okay, Samara? You look a little flushed."

He worked his fingers hard into Asia and in a moment she was writhing on his fingers, biting her knuckle to keep from screaming as she came on his hand.

"I think we're done here," I said, but waited for him to tell me it was okay to leave.

"You may be," Neil said with a smile. "But I think Asia and I are just getting started." With his free hand he grabbed a business card and held it out for me, two fingers on his other hand still buried inside Asia. "Samara, if you ever need anything, feel free to give me a call. I mean it. Anything."

He winked and with that I got up and turned to leave, wanting to get far away from his office and from whatever was about to happen between him and the waitress. I took a small detour, careful about where I was going this time and found the nearest ladies' room. Hurrying inside, I closed the door behind me and locked it. It was a single bathroom, probably meant only for staff and I was grateful for the moment of privacy.

What had I just witnessed and why was it making me feel this way? I tried to push the feelings aside, but I was so turned on and I knew there was no way I was going to finish my shift with this ache building in me.

My nipples were hard as rocks and I gave them each a hard pinch through my blouse. It felt good, but I could only imagine what it would have felt like to have Neil or even Asia's lips wrapped around the tightening flesh.

I hiked my skirt up and reach into my panties, finding them soaking wet and feeling for my swollen throbbing clit. Without holding back I stroked myself hard and fast and it didn't take very long for me to feel the warmth of an orgasm begin and then crash over me with a gasp. I watched myself in the mirror and thought how lucky any of those men upstairs would be to have me, even though I knew I'd never do such a thing.

I washed my hands and put myself back together and headed back out to the bar. There I found an exasperated Celeste. But Neil hadn't lied. She had a few bottles of vermouth in her possession and now all the guys who wanted to pretend they were James Bond were sated and happy with martinis in their hands. When Celeste caught sight of me she narrowed her eyes.

"I was with Neil—Mr. Vance."

I didn't realize those were the magic words, but Celeste's face softened and she nodded, but there was still a questioning look in her eyes.

"Is everything okay?"

I gave her an affirmative nod. "Yeah, it is. Sorry about the vermouth. There was a bit of a mixup."

Celeste brushed it off and together we finished the rest of the Saturday night shift. I had never been so happy to be done with work and heading back home to Jersey as I was that next morning with the dawn creeping in over the horizon.

## 5

I stepped into the glass shower and under the hot spray, reveling in the sheets of hot water that coursed down my skin. I let the water wash over my face, pondering the thoughts of what it would be like to give up my virginity, marveling about it every other day after what I had seen at Club V in NYC. I couldn't shake the image from my mind. Reaching out, I began to wash my hair, working the shampoo into a rich, foamy lather amidst my long locks. I closed my eyes and began to hum an old song when the noise from the shower muffled the sound of the bathroom door.

Almost, but not quite.

I kept my eyes closed as I heard the glass door swing open with the smallest click and then it closed again. Strong hangs began to caress my body, rubbing scented moisturizing body wash across the length and width of my body. Every part of me was suddenly on fire in the wake of the strong roving hands. I was instantly wet, a heat wholly unrelated to the water now flooding between my thighs.

It was him.

I had imagined his touch before.

I craved it.

I pushed my ass back slightly, and was rewarded - much to my titillating surprise - by a light stroke of his tongue against my tight bud. I shuddered with delight; he had to be kneeling behind me.

I was greedy for the feeling of his tongue working itself against my anus. I moaned with pleasure as he ran one strong hand up my thigh to rest on my vulva, his thumb firmly ensconced between my labia.

Oh god!

His touch felt so good. I placed both against the wall and spread my legs further apart, the better to give him access to my pussy. His tongue never ceased its slow torment, pressing it against my tight hole, seeking entry, only to pull back with a series of light licks.

My nipples were hard pebbles that ached, a sure sign that an orgasm was coming. Long locks hung down my face, moving in exaggerated time to the way I tossed my head with the pleasure he caused.

His thumb never moved, so I began to move against it, working in time with his tongue, savoring the way his digit grazed against my swelling clit.

Oh fuck. I was so close.

My breath began to come in ragged pants, and my hips began to buck of their own volition. My moans were loud now, unrestrained by any need to behave myself for him. I was now simply a creature of pure desire.

Somehow, he knew that, because he stood and pushed into me, the hard, thick length of his cock filling me so abruptly, stretching my virgin walls, that I cried out as the pleasure of my orgasm tore through my body.

I leaned against the wet tiled wall for support, my knees weak from the sensation as my body heaved with pleasure. He began to move in and out of me, purposefully denying me of any relief from the powerful sensations coursing through me through his own actions. It was driving me towards a new orgasm.

The worst and best part of it all was that he seemed totally immune to this intoxicating pleasure that we had achieved. I tried to outlast him but never even came close. By the time he so much as broke a sweat I was begging for another orgasm...for the second time.

As I clutched the tiled wall, my pussy throbbed with need and pleasure, the smell of sex mingling with the hot mist of the shower and I wondered how did he know how to manipulate my body like this? I didn't really care, as long as I came again.

He moved within me slowly, deliberately, using his cock to stroke my inner walls, skirting the limits of my receding orgasm, denying me of any break in the sensation while avoiding over stimulation.

Fuck it felt so good and I needed release now but it was clear he wasn't going to give it to me. With one hand on my clit, his index finger now firmly on top of my swollen clit, and his other on my hip for support, he was well positioned to torment me like this for hours. I knew that regardless of what my body craved, he would be perfectly content to keep me in this post-orgasmic state for another hour, until I had been reduced to a whimpering wreck, begging for release.

His finger tapped my clit a few times and I swear I saw stars. Fuck it felt incredible but I needed to come again. But here, now, with his cock buried to its hilt in my wet sopping cunt, my ears full of the sound of my own gasps and moans, his hands on me, guiding me around the sweet release of my own pleasure rather than to it, I knew that I could not achieve that relief.

My body ached and shivered with delight that he was deliberately denying my release. He was showing me how to completely surrender myself to him.

That he controlled my body in every way, just with a single touch. I rested my face against the cool tile and realized there was only one thing left to do in order to get release.

Beg.

My eyes flew open as the sunlight clawed its way

into my consciousness, forcing myself out of my dream. Jesus Christ! I'd been fucking dreaming again, entranced with the most exciting sex I had ever had. I smiled in my pillow, this one had been one hell of a dream and my panties were sopping wet. I had come in my sleep. Damn it. These dreams had been taking up occupancy in my mind now since I had seen the auction room. That girl on display for all to see.

It was time that I got a fucking grip on reality or I was going to lose my mind!

---

Six months later not much had changed at the Club V location in Jersey. I was still going in every day that I had a shift, running the bar when Suzy wasn't there and running it with her when she was. We were a dream team as far as the management was concerned and both of us had seen great raises over the time we had spent there.

"I'm not sure how I'll ever move on to a job in the corporate world. They don't tip you there, do they?" Suzy asked with a laugh and a frown.

"They might not tip you, but sometimes you get a company car if you're really well behaved. Oh, and Christmas bonuses!"

"Okay, now it's sounding better."

"But in that setting people aren't allowed to put $50

between your breasts. Or if they do, you get to take them to court and turn it into $500,000."

Suzy laughed again. "Seriously, Samara, you're selling me on this corporate life."

"Ladies, it is not all it's cracked up to be," Tommy Rollins chimed in from the other side of the bar. "No matter what it looks like, trust me, there is another side to the story. You know, you think you see all these people...all these people that crowd in here every weekend, and you think they've got it all. I'll tell you what. These people ain't got Jack Shit."

Tommy Rollins, top investment banker, was drunk at my bar for the fifth time in as many weeks. I didn't know what was up with the guy, as I had been trying to limit my personal conversations with him, but it was clear that something wasn't working out for him either at home or at work. I guessed it was the latter and I didn't want to ask. He was involved with a lot of very important people and on the off chance that something related to his business was about to go south, I didn't want to end up in a situation where I had to testify as to what Tommy Rollins had revealed while sitting on a bar stool.

"No one in here has nothing..." his words were slurring together. "Maybe you two," he said as he turned back to Suzy and I and regarded us thoughtfully. "Yeah, if I had to guess I would say that you two are probably the richest people in here. You got a family you love?"

Suzy was moving on to another customer and not taking the bait. It left me to deal with Tommy alone.

I nodded at him. "Yeah, I do."

He raised his glass. "Good for you. You know what I have? Fuck all. I used to have a wife and we had a baby…and then the baby, she died. And my wife couldn't deal with it. Or rather, I wasn't 'there for her' and she went back to her mom in Toronto. I mean, fuck's sake lady, what do you want me to do? Hold you while you cry or pay for all the shit you insist on having to live?"

I gave him a pitying half smile. "I'm sorry, Tommy. I didn't know about the baby."

"Not a lot you can do," he said. "Babies die. Weird, isn't it? Like they are there and they are so small and you'll do anything to take care of them but they are so tiny and what do you even do to keep them alive? Then one day you wake up, like you have every day before that for your entire fucking forty years on this earth… but your baby doesn't. Like, what the fuck, God?"

I had considered cutting him off and calling him a cab, but after hearing that I didn't have the heart. I had no idea how recent the loss might have been.

"This one is on me, Tommy." I said, sliding another scotch his way. "Just take it easy, okay? I don't want to have to worry about you getting home safely or not looking after yourself."

He looked like he was about to tear up and I fumbled to find some napkins in case he needed them.

"Samara, sweetheart. Just promise me this: Do whatever it takes to keep your family together. I don't care how hard it is, nothing is worse than being alone in this world. Things get ripped away from you and you might have no control over the situation, but when you do—for god's sake do whatever you have to for your family."

I nodded quickly and moved down the bar to help another club member. It wasn't often that I had these kinds of conversations at my bar. After all, we were a sex club. There was no mistaking that when you walked out on the floor. But the barstools tended to be filled by people who were sitting on the outside edge of all of this sex and excitement. It was as if they wanted to be a part of it, but somehow something in them kept them from being fully present and taking advantage of the situation. Which was a real shame considering the premium they were paying to walk through the door and sit and be served drinks by me.

I was getting a little introspective where I stood drying some glasses behind the bar. Maybe all that stuff about standing on the outside and not participating was something I should think about in my own life. I was spending so much time on work and school that there was a lot I was missing out on. There was a chance I needed to heed my own words and start applying them to my life if I was going to be handing out this kind of advice from behind my bar.

"How's Tommy?" Suzy asked as she came to stand

beside me. "That looked like it was about to go right down the toilet."

"Yeah, I think it's okay now. I'm a little worried about him, but he seems to at least have a good handle on what's important in life. I just had no idea he had been through that kind of trauma."

Suzy looked out across the room at our Friday night crowd. It was pretty tame for the moment but would undoubtedly get rowdier as the evening went on.

"You just never know what people are carrying with them."

I nodded and suddenly felt my phone vibrate. I didn't often receive calls while I was at work, so I reached for the phone and saw that it was my mom.

"That's weird," I said under my breath. "Suzy, I'm going to take this. Be back in a second."

I rounded the corner and answered the call.

"Hey Mom, what's up?"

"Honey, you need to get to the hospital. Your brother collapsed during his football game and they've rushed him to the emergency room. We're here now and I'm...I'm not sure what they're going to do..."

"What?! Mom, I'll be right there. Is Dad with you?"

"He's in the room with Josh right now. Your brother is conscious again, but they are going to take him back for some tests. Things are really up in the air right now and we don't want to leave him alone. If you can get out of work I think it would be best if you could get here...soon, honey."

I ended the call and headed back around to the bar. My emotions must have been showing all over my face because Suzy realized immediately that something was very wrong.

"What's happened? Do you need to leave?" She asked, her voice full of concern.

"Yeah," my voice came out thick and cracking. I nodded my head. "Yes, I've got to go. It's my brother. Don't know what's going on but he collapsed during his football game and now they've got him at the emergency room. My mom...my mom seems to think I need to be there so..."

"Go, get out of here now. Get your purse and go."

In a daze I stumbled down the hallway to the dressing room and grabbed my things from my locker before rushing out of the club and out to my car.

It all happened so quickly from there. I had no memory of the route I took to the hospital. It was all muscle memory from when I had driven every day to see my grandfather. All the way there the only thing I could think about was how much I loved my brother and how I would do anything in the world to make sure he was okay. He was such a strong, fun guy. Always in the middle of something, always making people laugh. People couldn't help but smile whenever Josh was around and everyone loved him.

The thought of him lying there in a hospital bed,

prone and with tubes and wires connected to him terrified me. He was my little brother, although we weren't that far apart in age. Sure we had fought like cats and dogs growing up, but the truth was that he was my closest family member. There wasn't anything I wouldn't do to try to make life easier for him.

Tommy's words came back to me and I shuddered. It was too eerie to have just had that conversation and then be faced with potential tragedy.

"Please, let him be okay," I said aloud to the air as I sped along the road to the hospital.

I arrived, hardly knowing how I had gotten there at all, and parked in the emergency room parking area. Running up to the automatic doors I waited as they opened slowly and cursed them as I bolted into the waiting area of the emergency room.

Neither of my parents were in sight so I made my way to the front desk.

"Josh...Tanza," I said, only then realizing I was out of breath.

The nurse looked up from her computer. "Take a deep breath honey. Are you okay? Do you need to see a doctor?"

I shook my head, exasperated and struggling to find the words I needed in the moment. It was all too much and I was overwhelmed, not knowing where my parents were or how Josh was doing.

"My brother. An ambulance brought my brother

here." I took another deep breath. "He collapsed at his football game."

That seemed to ring a bell and she nodded and pointed down a hallway. "Football player, that's right. Curtain three. It should be fine for you to go in there now."

I hurried down the hall and read the numbers that were posted above the different curtained sections of the emergency room area. I reached Curtain three and to my surprise, it was empty and there were fresh new sheets on this bed. I whirled around, shocked and scared at what this might mean, but thankfully a nurse standing nearby read the situation and rushed over to me.

"Looking for the football player?"

I nodded affirmatively at her.

"It's okay, they've moved him up to the third floor. If you'll just head up there and check at the nurse's station they'll be able to send you to him.

I felt like it was all taking too long. I just wanted to get to Josh's side and make sure everything was going to be okay. At this point I had no idea what was going on, what had really happened, or if he was in any immediate danger. The fact that he had been moved to a real room didn't give me any comfort and I wondered what on earth it could all be about as I raced back down the hall and into one of the elevators.

The third floor was a flurry of activity and I was deposited right outside of the nurse's station.

"Excuse me, my brother is Josh Tanza. I was told he's up here." I looked around at the nurses behind the desk and waited for one of them to show me a little mercy.

One of the male nurses nodded. "Yeah, the football player. He's in 308."

Now certain where my brother was, I was in less of a hurry because I wasn't sure what I was walking into. My mom hadn't had the time to explain everything on the phone and now I had to face the fact that Josh was really, truly ill.

The door was open and a doctor was exiting the room as I approached it. My parents were standing on either side of Josh's bed and my brother was lying there, hooked up to several different monitors, looking so pale you would have thought he had either seen a ghost or somehow morphed into a Casper-like version of himself.

"Oh my god, Josh." I rushed to my mother's side but hesitated before leaning in to hug my brother, opting instead to squeeze his hand. He made a strong fist, but not nearly as strong as I knew he was capable of and that concerned me.

"Honey, I'm so glad you're here," my mom said as she embraced me. My dad came around to hug us both tightly while Josh looked up from his hospital bed with a slight grin on his face.

"You guys having fun?" He asked.

I rolled my eyes at him. "Hey dude, you be nice.

You've got us all worried. What's going on with you?" I posed the question to my mom and dad as much as to Josh.

"We're still waiting to hear a few results from the doctor," my dad said calmly. He looked rough, like whatever he had watched happen to my brother on the football field had taken some years off of his life. For all I knew it might have.

Josh didn't look well. He was pale and his skin was clammy and although I knew he hated it, I kept checking his temperature with the back of my hand.

"You're too cold, Josh."

"You're telling me," he shot back. "And they won't let me wear a shirt yet. I've got to stay hooked up to all of these things for a while."

"Well, they've got to find out what's going on. My guess is that a cheeseburger is to blame for it. Somehow, someway, it's a cheeseburger."

"Ha-ha," Josh said, not finding the remark humorous in the least. "For your information I have been eating a healthy, protein-filled diet. Trying to keep myself lean."

He didn't look lean though. He looked puffy, like he had consumed just a little too much sodium. I was worried, less so than I had been on the way over, but still enough that I made a conscious effort to hide the emotion from my face as much as possible.

"Mom, Dad, do you guys need anything? I could go

get you some snacks or a coffee or something. Whatever you need."

My mom shook her head. "Gerry and I want to stay here so that we don't miss the doctor. There's no need for you to go to any trouble for us."

"It's no trouble at all, Mom. Really, I would be happy to do something for you." I paused then, listening to myself, taking a moment to understand that what I was truly doing was making an attempt to rescue myself from the proceedings going on right now with my family. It was hard to be in the room, to see my little brother hooked up to these machines and absolutely helpless. This wasn't the way that things were supposed to be, not for someone his age with so much promise in his life. Josh had a future in front of him, one that was looking bright. How was it possible for him to be facing something of this magnitude, whatever it was?

I felt the tears welling in my eyes and I moved away from the bed to sit in one of the chairs in the room, burying my face in my hands. It was ignorant and silly to be questioning all of this. Of course something like this could be happening to my family—people encountered these things every day and we were no different. It was only that it had been so long since we had seen any kind of tragedy and none of it had ever been in my immediate family. What I was dealing with was ignorance and a sort of privilege—I had never had to witness a health crisis like this and now that one was right in the middle of my family, it was like a bomb had gone off. It was only that now I was close enough to feel the impact of such a thing.

My dad came over and put his arm around my shoulder and comforted me while I cried. This wasn't about me, but I had to get the emotions out. I wanted the same thing my parents wanted—to find out what was going on with Josh and to make sure we did whatever it took to see him well again.

6

It felt like ages waiting for one of the doctors to come back in with some test results to discuss with us. For a moment we started to wonder if it would be during the next morning's rounds, but all of us knew we weren't going anywhere until we had some word about Josh's condition.

One of the doctor's had come in during the middle of the night to go over the event that happened to Josh on the football field.

"It was, technically speaking, a heart attack," he said.

I gripped my mom's arm, steeling myself as much as making sure she wasn't going to collapse right there beside Josh's bed.

"What? It can't be." My dad was beside himself. "He's only 17…I've heard of that sort of thing, but isn't that rare?"

The doctor made a kind of pained face. "Well, it all depends on the sort of event that led to the heart attack. So that's what we're looking at now. While most of these things can be spotted easily after an event like this, Josh's was a pretty minor thing—all things considered. It's the sort of thing some people experience and are often able to go on about their day though in some terrible discomfort. In a way he was lucky that he lost consciousness, but that adds another element to it."

"So, when will we know something concrete?" My mom asked.

"I've handed this over to one of my colleagues who has a little more experience with pediatric cardiac events such as this. Your son, while almost a grown man, is still technically a kid. What he has going on here is likely something that has been going on for a while. What we're looking at now is the cause of the event and what we can do to prevent another one from happening."

I listened intently as the doctor spoke, not wanting to miss a word. Both of my parents were so caught up in all of this that I knew it could be valuable for me to be their ears in these situations. Sometimes it was easy to miss out on a word here or there or misinterpret what the doctors were saying.

"For instance," the doctor went on, "if Josh were a 45-year-old, beer-guzzling, pizza eating contest winning guy who looked like he was carrying around a keg in his gut, I would have a pretty clear guess as to what the cause of his issues were. However, Josh is 17 and that on its own makes this a significantly murkier case to look at. He's healthy by all accounts, was playing football when this happened, and I'm guessing has been going to two-a-day practices since late summer?"

Josh nodded, finally entering into the discussion about his health.

"Ever had any chest pains during practice, Josh?"

He shook his head. "Nah, I mean…nothing more than usual. Like, not my chest but in my stomach. But that's just the normal thing. We run so much we puke in the early days of practice. I'm just like every other guy on my team as far as that goes."

The doctor marked something on a clip board. "Do you ever feel out of breath for no good reason?"

Josh thought about it for a moment. "Well, I had asthma when I was little and sometimes I feel like that is flaring up."

That statement caught the doctor's attention. "Okay, that right there is the sort of thing I'm looking for in a person's medical history. It's the kind of thing that people tend to forget. You don't think about him having asthma when he was little and then when similar symptoms crop back up when he's 17, he just thinks it's a touch of the asthma coming back. The truth of that is—and this is just me hypothesizing and in no way a diagnosis—the way your bronchial tubes work and where they are placed, when there is stress on them and you're having an asthma attack or something close to one it can feel like tightening along with the shortness of breath. Does that sound like what you've been experiencing?"

Josh nodded and looked back and forth between my parents.

"So the thing with that is—a lot of things can feel like an asthma attack. Now it's usually the reverse happening, like someone coming in with tightness in their chest and shortness of breath, thinking they have had a heart attack. In those cases it's usually something else—like a panic attack, asthma, costochondritis, or any number of conditions than can occur in the chest wall. In your situation, however, I believe we have a cardiac event or condition that has been masking itself as your asthma symptoms returning to haunt you."

It was all a lot to take in and the doctor left us with that information to digest for a few hours before his colleague followed up.

At nearly dawn, the specialist came in and he was much more abrupt in tone than the other doctor had been.

"Josh, Mr. and Mrs. Tanza, I'm Dr. Douglas and I'm going to cut right to the chase here."

None of us had gotten much sleep in the hospital room and bleary-eyed we looked at the doctor awaiting what he had to say about Josh's prognosis and recovery.

"I was able to look at the images we got of Josh's

heart and I have been monitoring all the information these machines have gathered throughout the night." He tapped one of the machines that was connected to Josh with several different wires. "It took some real searching, but I was able to locate the source of the problem. Josh has got a very tiny hole in his heart."

My mother gasped audibly and held onto my father's hand for dear life.

"Typically that is the sort of thing that rights itself as the kid grows. In some cases it becomes a situation that needs to be rectified with surgery. In even rarer cases though we see situations where, because the issue has gone on so long unchecked—or because of other reasons in this case—that surgery doesn't appear to be an option."

"What do you mean—you can't perform surgery to fix this problem?" My dad asked, astonished.

Dr. Douglas shook his head. "I'm afraid not. What was found near the hole was something more serious. Josh's heart is severely malformed. One of the chambers is larger than it is supposed to be. It's pumping blood in a way that is very difficult for the rest of his heart to keep up with. That, combined with the hole, has made a very serious situation indeed. I don't want to alarm you, but the truth is that this is a very grave situation and you need to know it now so you are prepared to make the decisions that are going to happen in front of you in the coming days."

I sat there in shock, not entirely sure what the

doctor was going to tell us next. What it sounded like from here was that there wasn't anything he could do to help my brother and that thought was enough to knock me sideways.

"What I'm saying is...that it's a miracle Josh is here today. He shouldn't be, frankly. It's the sort of thing that might show up in an infant or not and they might be dead the next day. It's astounding that something hasn't happened before now. But here we are and you've got to think about some things. Josh is young, so he'll be moved up the list, and he's healthy so that's also in his favor."

"Wait, what? Are you talking about a transplant?" Josh blurted out.

Dr. Douglas nodded. "I'm afraid that is our only option here, Josh. There might be a possibility of repairing the hole in your heart, but given the severity of the malformation it is unlikely that surgery would make much difference. If you want any chance of living out your adult life, we're going to have to get you a new heart."

It was then that I thought I was going to pass out. I took a deep breath as the news began to sink in with all of my family members and I silently prayed that this would all work out, somehow.

---

It took a week to hear back from the insurance

company. We knew what the cost was going to be now and the first thing Suzy did for me was to start a fundraiser so that we could pay the medical bill for Josh's new heart.

Hearing the amount it was going to cost after all the insurance would cover was terribly disheartening and I didn't know how we would ever manage it. It was a debt that my parents would be saddled with for the rest of their lives. Any hope they might have had of retiring was snuffed out of sight, because they would pay every last cent they had to make sure that their child had the medical care he needed to survive, like any parent would.

I cursed the state of American healthcare and buried my face in my hands in the dressing room of Club V. I was on my break and had just gotten off the phone with my mom who was getting ready for whenever they would eventually receive the call that Josh was getting a transplant. It was something that worried her, the thought that someone else was going to have to die to give Josh a chance to live. She was coming to terms with it though and had accepted that somehow, something good was going to come out of all of this.

"Hey," Suzy said as she came up behind me and rubbed my back. "How are you doing?"

I sighed and shrugged. "I would be a lot better if my lotto winnings decided to show up. You know, the lotto winnings to the lottery that I never remembered to enter."

"Ah yes, that one. Yeah, I'm waiting on those to come in as well." She looked at me, pity clear in her eyes. "I wish there was something I could do to help you out, Samara."

"Suzy, you have done so much already to help with the fundraising. Really, I can't thank you enough." I took a deep breath. "It's just that it won't ever be enough. I've decided to give my parents all that I have saved to go toward Josh's surgery."

"Seriously?" She looked shocked at this admission.

I nodded. "I don't have nearly enough, but even the smallest amount helps. Twenty-thousand is all that I have saved, which I know is a lot, considering, but it'll hardly touch this. I just have no idea how we're going to come up with $150,000. I've got to find some way to get this money and fast. Seriously, I'll do anything to get the amount they need, but I just have no idea how to accomplish it. I think it might be impossible."

Suzy looked a little sheepish then, like she was keeping something from me. We had known each other for far too long for her to start keeping secrets now.

"What?" I asked. "I know that look on your face. You can't hide anything from me. Cough it up, now."

Suzy bit her lip. "Okay, I'll tell you, but I want you to promise you aren't going to hate me or get mad at me over this. Okay?"

I reached out and grabbed her hand gently. "Suzy, never. You're my best friend. What's up?"

"I was thinking about how you might be able to get some cash fast and seriously, Samara, if I could do it myself then I would, but unfortunately that ship sailed a long time ago."

I shot her a funny look. "What are you talking about?"

She cleared her throat and braced herself to say something that was clearly difficult for her to verbalize.

"I'm talking about 'The Room'. The one you saw in New York."

The Room was enough, she didn't have to clarify any further than that. I took another deep breath.

"I would be lying if I said it hadn't crossed my mind," I admitted in a hushed tone.

Suzy gave my hand a squeeze. "Listen, Samara—there is nothing to be ashamed of. Honestly, I've never heard of a more admirable reason to do something like this. It would be to help your family and while I in no way think you need to feel pressure to help them financially, if this is something you are committed to doing...then this is an option."

I nodded and stared at my hands. From the moment I first heard the amount that my parents were going to have to pay for my brother's transplant surgery, the thought of the auction block at Club V NYC had been floating there in the back of my mind like a specter. As much as I had been averse to the idea when I first encountered it in the flesh, now that it was my brother's life I was taking into consideration, there were a lot of things I would do to make sure that he got the care he needed.

"Yeah, honestly I am glad you brought it up. I have really been thinking about it and sort of asking the universe for a sign. I know you probably don't want to be that for me," I said with a reassuring smile, "but I think I'm going to pretend that you are."

"Samara, seriously, you don't have to do this. But I do want you to know that you have my full support if it's the route you want to take. There is nothing to be ashamed of here. It's your body and you can do what you want with it. And you know what? I bet since you're an employee here already they will do some... what is that called? 'Extreme vetting' for you." She couldn't keep herself from giggling. "Seriously though, Stew loves you to death and would never let you end up in a bad situation. He's close with the folks in New York. Let him make a few calls and get the thing set up if you want to do it. I bet they can make sure that someone really nice is there for you. They won't let you go to any kind of sick fuck or someone that's into dishing out harsh BDSM."

The idea was really starting to take root in my brain now and I wondered exactly what kind of guy I would end up with. There would be no way of knowing beforehand, not even who would make up the group of people who would be there that night for the bidding. And that was if I could even make the cut for the auction block.

"What if they...don't want me?" I asked timidly. I didn't know what was coming over me in that moment, but something about it made me feel very vulnerable.

Suzy held onto my hands and pulled me up to my feet, then turned me around to face one of the full length mirrors.

"Look at yourself," she said softly. And I did, for the first time in a while I took a long look at myself in the mirror. My eyes were a little puffy from all the crying I had been doing over the past few weeks, but overall my face still looked pretty, young and fresh as it ever had.

"May I?" she asked and like that my best friends hands were on my body, running her long fingers down my curves as she whispered into my ear. "You've got a stunning figure and any man would be lucky to be with you. I think it's important that women tell their friends things like this. You are going to go up there and knock 'em dead, Samara. Mark my words."

---

Suzy went to Stew for me and had the first conversation broaching the subject. At first he hadn't wanted to discuss the matter at all, acting as if the auction block was only a myth or false rumors. But as she later told me, when she pressed him on it and told him about my run-in while I was at the New York location, he finally conceded. Still, he didn't want to let me go.

I went in for a meeting with him to discuss matters

and to help him eliminate any fears he may have had about letting me make this decision for myself.

"Let me be clear, Stew, I am not talking about working the floor. That's not on the table for me."

"You're damn right it's not," he seemed offended that I'd even consider it. Even though management at Club V was always open to us moving up the chain, Stew was very protective of his bar staff and it seemed like he had come to think of me as almost a daughter.

"Samara, I just need to know this is something you really want to do. I understand what a sensitive topic it is and how uncomfortable you might feel talking to me about it."

I sat across from Stew at his desk. I didn't often venture into this room, but it was clear that the guy behind the desk was one of the good ones. A family man who was looking out for his people, he only wanted the best for me.

"Stew, I assure you I came to this decision on my own. My family needs my help now more than ever and if I can do this for them then I feel like I would be a fool to pass it up. I don't feel like I'm holding on to anything anymore. This would simply be a transaction. And I'm guessing the club would act as the broker here?"

My boss nodded and sighed. "But let's get this clear —I'm getting you the best price I can. They're fair, I suppose, don't get me wrong about that. I'd never tarnish the name of Club V. I just don't want you to end up getting a deal that isn't a good one. And you aren't going home with one of those sick fucks either. No, I will make sure personally that whoever has the option of bidding on you will be the top of the line...like, marriage material. Samara, do you think I could just set you up with someone and you guys could get married?"

I laughed at him. He was clearly still very troubled by the idea of me selling my virginity.

"Stew, while that is a very generous offer, I'm afraid that I'm here for the money and not a husband or true love. Just make sure he's decent and then I guess I'll take it from there."

My boss nodded and let out a long exhale. "Okay then. If you're set on doing it then I don't suppose there's any way of talking you out of it. I'll make a call and get the ball rolling. You should know something before the end of the week."

---

It didn't take that long to get an answer from the New York club. It was a quick and definite, YES. Stew told me to expect a call from Elle and like clockwork it came the next day.

"Samara? Hi, it's Elle. I'm the staffing director...we met back when you worked here one night."

"Right, of course. Thanks for calling, Elle." I heard

a nervous edge in my voice and tried to push any of the nerves I was feeling out of my mind.

"We're so happy that you've decided to come on board with the club in this capacity. However, given the sensitive nature of this business, I'm going to have to ask that you come to the New York club so that we can talk about this in person and get things all set up. How does tomorrow afternoon sound to you?"

"Great, I can be there whenever you need me."

We set up an appointment for 2:00pm the following afternoon and I made my way to the city the same way I had six months prior. I had less trepidation this time around, which was odd considering what I was going to the club to discuss. I had a lot of thoughts swirling in my mind and my only hope for the day was that I would not come face to face with Neil Vance.

I was buzzed in and Elle greeted me at the door before leading me back to her office. It was a bright, open space, so unlike the rest of the establishment and I immediately felt reassured and at home in her presence. She was dressed in a tight black dress this time around, still professional but enticing enough to make her fit right in at Club V.

Elle took a seat behind her desk and invited me to make myself comfortable across from her. She flashed me a genuine, beaming smile as she spoke.

"Honestly, Samara, I am so glad that you have come to us with this. I know it can be a very sensitive thing to discuss and I understand if you feel a little weird about it, but I want you to know that you can trust me and that this is all done with the utmost discretion."

I nodded. "I've been assured that this is the place to go if I am looking to...sell these sorts of goods."

She laughed good-humoredly. "You're funny. That's good. It's really important to have a sense of humor going into this. It helps to keep things a little lighter, I think. To get down to business though—you are a virgin, correct?"

"Yes. I was under the impression that was a requirement."

"Oh, it is for this, however I was just going to let you know that I'll spare you the medical verification. You're an employee and you've been with us for a while and I've been assured that you are trustworthy. Now, here's the part where I would typically ask you about your interests and what you are okay with and not okay with and all that jazz—however, we have a sort of unique situation here."

I was curious about what she could possibly mean. "Oh?"

"Well, it's not entirely unique. You see, sometimes we have men who speak up for women right away. These women never make it to the auction block. It isn't very common because we don't really like to do our business that way. It's better to bring them into the club, you know. We aren't just some virgin matchmaking service." She laughed. "This is about the Club

V experience. We want everyone to have the best time and we also want to maintain some of the mystique we've managed to build. Keeping the auctions in house and insisting that our bidders show up and participate in the event is one way of doing that."

It all made sense to me, but I still wasn't sure what she was talking about when she said there was a unique situation.

"What I'm saying is that you will not be going on the auction block."

"What?" My eyes went wide, stunned. Hadn't she just told me that they were thrilled to have me here for this?

"Oh, you're still going to be matched and receive your fee," she said, as if she could hear my inner monologue. "You just won't appear for auction. Look at it this way, it's fewer people who get to see you naked. Personally, I'm convinced that some of those guys just come for the show. We boot browsers out after a few times though. No, you've already been matched. Someone saw your photo come up in the listing of women who were soon to be up for auction and he requested to have you taken down immediately and put on reserve for him."

I swallowed hard. This had all happened very quickly and now I was faced with the fact that it was very real and was going to happen soon.

"Wow, I guess I'm flattered." I didn't know what else to say about the matter.

"Yes, well, like I said it is pretty rare, but sometimes we make allowances for really good clients. I even let him know of the specific situation we are dealing with here—I am so sorry about your brother, by the way. But I let them know that we had a hard minimum on the fee. This person countered that offer."

"Countered it with what?"

She slid a stack of papers across the desk to me. "As you know the length of our contracts can vary, with some of our individuals who are auctioned going for up to a year."

I gulped. "Someone could buy me for a year?"

She shook her head, "They could, but they didn't. Don't worry. That is usually limited to royalty from certain countries several thousands of miles away. You're not going overseas."

"Thank goodness," I said, breathing a sigh of relief as I looked at the documents.

"This person offered terms and I'll explain them to you now so you don't have to worry about reading all fifty pages there. That's just to say that you agree to everything and it's a binding contract between you and the buyer and that Club V is only acting as an intermediary between two consenting adult parties who are engaging in legal activities."

I nodded as I took it all in. It was a lot for one afternoon.

"The terms that this person offered are very simple. You will be at their disposal for one week. If you agree, then the contract will start this Saturday at 7:00 pm in the evening. His counter offer was, I quote, 'To pay her brother's medical bills in their entirety.'"

I dropped the pen I had been holding in my hand as I looked over the documents and looked up at Elle with what must have been complete and utter shock written all over my face.

"I know," she said with a soft smile. "It's a very generous offer. This includes all billing for your brother's transplant surgery and whatever happens during his recovery. I really couldn't believe it myself, but this is a very special sort of client and he seemed keen whenever he got a look at you."

"I really don't know what to say, Elle." I didn't know what to say, but I knew what I was thinking. There was no turning back now. No matter what the rest of the terms were, I was going to take this man up on his offer because there was no way I could get a better deal than this. If it was about helping my family then this was the ultimate—the ideal situation that I could find myself in. Only a fool would refuse an offer like this.

"There's just one more thing you need to know before we get to the boring legal stuff. Their one stipulation was that you would not find out who they are until you arrive at the place you'll be staying for the week. Rest assured that this person has been thoroughly checked out and that you'll be in good hands here. Totally safe." She smiled again, a clear attempt to make sure that I felt comfortable. "So you'll be picked up on Saturday evening and taken to the place where you'll be spending your week with this individual. You'll meet him there and then...things will go from there. This is lined out in more detail in the paperwork, but I'll explain in simple terms for you here." Elle cleared her throat. "While no one is expected to be coerced into anything or to participate in any act that they feel uncomfortable with, it is imperative that you understand you are agreeing to full sexual intercourse to completion with this individual at least once in the span of the week. That is all you are legally required to do when you sign this document. I will say that since you have been purchased for the week that slightly more is typically expected, but that is to be discussed between you and your buyer. If you fail to perform this one act that you are agreeing to in this document, you will forfeit all profit and Club V will not be expected to pay you anything. Do you understand?"

I understood completely, but something didn't sit well with me. "What if the person were to lie to get out of paying?"

She nodded and grinned. "Our clients are thoroughly vetted. I can't say we've ever had that happen, but trust me that we have doctors on call who will perform an exam if that is necessary. Just make sure and let us know if you think there is going to be an issue."

I leafed through the paperwork and listened as Elle continued talking. It all looked like it was in really good order and I had faith that I wasn't walking into this totally blind. Club V had a reputation to uphold and they valued the women who put themselves up for auction as many of them continued to come back as club members with their buyers or other people from the club.

"I think you'll find, and you may already know from working with us, that we are a family here and we take care of our own. Trust me, Samara. You are going to be well taken care of. And I hope we continue to see you around Club V NYC for years to come."

With that we went through the legal documents and she explained them all to me very carefully. Something made me think it probably would have been a good idea to have an attorney present for something like what I was signing, but I didn't have the time or the funds for that kind of nonsense. No, instead I was signing my virginity away and by Sunday morning all of that would be taken care of and I would have a week of...who knew exactly—maybe intense sexual awakening. I signed my name on the final page and with that it was done.

## 7

"One whole week with this guy? Samara, what if he's like, Slender Man or something?" Suzy said as she watched me from the comfort of her bed.

I elbowed her out of the way as I started to pack a bag. I had no idea what I was going to need for the week, so I packed an assortment of things that I thought would get me through the days I was with this person, wherever they lived. It seemed like they must be within driving distance based on what little information Elle had given me, but beyond that I had no clue.

"Yuck. Thanks a lot, Suzy. Now I'm not going to be able to sleep tonight. Besides, I get the feeling this is a city guy and I don't think the city is Slender Man's natural habitat. Also, let's not forget that you are the one who suggested this."

She shot me a searing glare. "Hey now, you're an

adult woman who decided to do this on her own. You have free will!"

"I know, I know. I'm only kidding. You know I decided to do this myself. And honestly, I'm kind of looking forward to it."

"You aren't scared or anything?" Her voice was quieter as she asked the question.

I took a deep breath as I looked down at the clothes in my bag. "I would be lying if I said I wasn't a little scared. It's something new for me and I feel sort of weird being nineteen and still being a virgin. It's like something that's a part of me, but also not a big deal at all? I don't know, it's weird. Like it is something that society has made to seem so important when in reality it's just this little blip on the radar when it comes down to it. No one really ever talks about guys losing their virginity like it is some sort of monumental act. But here I am, selling mine to literally the highest bidder."

"In fairness, we don't know what you would have brought on that auction block," she said with a laugh.

"I don't think it would be as much as I'm assured to get now. Who would have ever thought I would find someone who wanted to pay my brother's entire bill for the transplant. Now the only thing to do is wait and pray for a heart to become available."

"And of course you have to hold up your end of the bargain," Suzy reminded me politely.

"As if I would back out now."

Our apartment buzzer went off then and Suzy went

to answer it while I continued packing and preparing for the week ahead of me. I would be picked up by car the following evening and driven to a destination I was unsure of. I wasn't worried too much about this aspect of it and Suzy had even offered to get in her car and tail us just so she would have some idea where I was being taken. I declined that offer, not wanting to infringe on the privacy of the club member.

The thought had crossed my mind that I might know this person. Whether from the club or somewhere else, the reason they picked me could have very well been based on how familiar my face was to them. It was a strange thing to consider, that this person I was about to hand over my virginity to could be someone I encountered in my daily life. At the very least I knew that they had to be a club member. The only question left was if they were a regular member at my location or one of the others. I would soon find out and all of my questions would be answered.

Suzy appeared in the bedroom doorway carrying a large manila envelope. "It's for you. Came by messenger."

"How odd," I said as I took the envelope and set aside the task of packing for a moment to see what had been delivered. There was no return address and the envelope had some bulk to it. I opened it carefully and slid out the contents. There was a wrapped package inside as well as a letter on fine stationary that suspiciously lacked any kind of letterhead or signature.

"What is it?" Suzy asked.

I skimmed the letter and looked up at Suzy when I was done, eyes wide. I read it aloud to her.

Dear Samara,

*I am looking forward to meeting you tomorrow. I thought you might be packing for the week so I wanted to enclose a few items that will be of use to you while you are with me.*

*You will wear the red items the first night you are with me. Wear them under the dress I am sending you. The dress will arrive separately later today. Put these items on to prepare for our first meeting.*

*As far as what you need to pack—leave everything at home. That is not a request, it is an order. No makeup, no toiletries—nothing. You will be completely catered to in my home.*

*It is my delight to have the pleasure of your companionship over the next week. I hope you are looking forward to this with as much anticipation as I am.*

The letter was unsigned.

"Jeez, he's a little demanding isn't he? What is it that he wants you to wear?"

I turned my attention to the package and opened it

up. Wrapped in thin tissue paper was some red lingerie—a barely there matching bra and panty set.

"A lot of support this will give me," I said, holding up the flimsy bra in front of my breasts.

Suzy shook her head. "Yeah, I don't think he cares. So, that's what you're going to wear under the dress. Wonder what that will look like? What else do you have there?"

There was a small white box inside the package, something that a bracelet or necklace might be packed in. I slowly lifted the lid and looked at the contents.

"Holy shit," Suzy said as she followed my gaze and looked into the box. "That's a dog collar."

It wasn't just any dog collar. The thing was encrusted with diamonds and a small metal plate that had my name engraved on it.

"Were you expecting a dog collar?" she asked cocking an eyebrow.

"Do I look like I was expecting one?" I pulled the item out of the box and examined it further.

"I mean, that is one hell of a piece of jewelry. I am pretty sure those are real diamonds. Do you think he expects you to show up to his place wearing it?"

I shook my head. "I don't care if he expects it or not, that wasn't in the contract and he didn't mention it in the letter, so I'll just pack it and hope that he forgets about it."

Suzy grimaced. "I think you're going to be wearing a dog collar before the week is out."

THE NEXT AFTERNOON rolled around and I got ready for my first evening. Now I was feeling the butterflies and there was no denying it. Suzy was already at work, which meant I would be alone when the driver arrived.

The dress had been delivered as promised the prior afternoon and Suzy and I had opened it, all the while wondering if it would be anything as outrageous as the dog collar. It wasn't, but we both saw that it was a designer dress, something that would sell for about $5000 in a boutique. It was tight and white, sleeveless, and with good portions cut out of both of the sides.

I was getting dressed and I was pleased to see how the dress looked on me. Somehow the guy had guessed my size perfectly and I was impressed by that particular skill. I would still have to see how he did in other areas.

Following my instructions, I packed only a small handbag worth of items, which included the collar. I wasn't completely opposed to wearing it, but I felt some uncertainty about the activities that often went along with an item like that. I was a virgin, but I wasn't completely inexperienced with men. There had been a lot of fooling around, hand jobs, blow jobs, and there was even one guy who had been really into spanking and being spanked. I didn't think that was my cup of tea, but it all could have been because he really sucked at it. Maybe this guy would be different. Hell, if he could afford to drop this kind of money on a virgin, a dress, and a dog collar, maybe he was up to the task.

It was nearing 6:00 pm that evening when the buzzer finally rang and I called down.

"Yes?"

"Samara Tanza? This is Dwight, your driver for the evening. I have the car here waiting out in front of the building if you'd like to come down."

"Be right there!" I called, a little too cheerily on second thought. There was nothing for me to grab other than my keys and phone, so I stuffed those things in my handbag and headed out the door.

Dwight was waiting at the door of my building and kindly opened the passenger door of the car to let me in.

"Thank you," I said.

"My pleasure," was Dwight's only answer before he went around the car to set off on our journey.

It was Saturday evening so traffic was a little different than it would be on a week day, but people were crowding into the city for weekend shows and dinners and we found ourselves sitting in traffic for much longer than I thought it would take us to get anywhere in the city. I heard Dwight make a call telling someone we would be running late and I strained to listen for the voice on the other line. There was nothing I could make anything of, just a non distinct male voice.

As we sat there in traffic my mind drifted back to

what I had seen the day I stumbled into the auction room at Club V in the city. Sure, it had been a shock to me but now I was a little less troubled by what the women were doing there. Each woman had her own story, her own reason for being there. I could hardly fault any of them for making decisions using their own free will, especially not now that I had had ended up in a predicament where I had a decision—to help my family or not. I made the choice freely, but deep in my heart I knew that there was no other way. I wanted to help my younger brother so desperately and this was the way I was going to do it.

We crept slowly into the city, finally making it to some major streets that I recognized. We were on our way into a very swanky area and I wondered just how much money this guy must have to be able to afford an apartment anywhere near this place.

Suddenly we stopped and Dwight called from the front, "This is it."

We were in front of a massive building and as Dwight opened the door for me, I looked up the height of the mirrored side. It was so tall, I felt a little dizzy just looking up at it.

"Miss Tanza, you'll just go in, give them your name at the desk, and they'll escort you to the elevator."

I nodded and entered the building, greeting the security guard at the desk. I had no idea who I was asking for, so I hoped that giving them my name alone would be enough to steer me in the right direction.

"Samara Tanza, someone is expecting me."

The security guard nodded. "Right this way." Instead of leading me to the main elevators, we went down a side hallway that opened up into another foyer with its own private entrance from a side street. He entered a code on a keypad outside the elevator and the doors opened. "Private elevator to the penthouse. Have a nice evening, Miss Tanza."

The penthouse.

Well, that answered all of my questions about how much money the guy had.

Answer: More than God.

The elevator whisked me up the side of the building like a rocket and I held onto one of the rails, less so because of the speed of the contraption and more because it was finally sinking in what I was walking into—and the truth was, I didn't know the half of it yet. I didn't know what this guy looked like or what he expected of me. If he was totally into the collar thing or if that had been some kind of joke. Maybe he was a nerdy type and was a little interested in trying something kinky that he had never done before. Getting off of that elevator I knew that what I was about to step into was wild and almost completely unknown. The only thing I was certain of was that I was about to walk through the door and meet that man who would rid me of my virginity.

The doors opened and I stepped out onto a slate gray marble floor. The entire foyer was covered in marble, from floor to ceiling, and the furniture that populated the area was covered in a fine white fabric. It was clearly the sort of furniture that no one ever used. There were exotic plants spread around the small room that opened up into a larger living area.

There was no sign of the occupant of the penthouse, so I walked slowly into the main living area, hoping to either be noticed or catch a glimpse of someone. The room was opulent and the ceilings were high. A fireplace was the centerpiece of the room and a small fire was burning there already. I was grateful for that as there was a chill in the air which was normal for early in the spring, but my dress didn't provide much shielding from that. There was a plate of cheese and crostini set out on a table and a bottle of champagne on ice. I wandered over to check out the label, not that I knew much about a good year for champagne, but I knew what the people who knew things about wine ordered at the bar. What I knew about this bottle was that it cost more than my dress. And maybe the dog collar, too.

"Samara."

His voice came from somewhere behind me and I turned with a start. The true shock was his face though, one I had not expected to see again, and possibly the last I wanted to see here, now.

Neil Vance.

8

"So good to see you again. I didn't anticipate the circumstances, but life is full of surprises."

The man was as cocky as he had been the first night I met him, but there was something a little different about him tonight. I couldn't put my finger on it. How on earth had it been Neil? I didn't have time to think through the whys and hows now though. I was in this for the long haul.

"Good evening," I said, playing it cool. I was certain he had read the look of shock and surprise on my face and that he was probably reveling in it silently.

"Thank you for having me here." I realized how dumb it sounded the minute the words left my lips, but I didn't know what else to say in the situation. Hey, thanks for paying to take my virginity and saving my little brother's life. That wouldn't have worked either, although it was closer to what I was feeling in the moment.

"On the contrary, it's my pleasure to have you here and I hope it will be yours as well, in time. Why don't we have a seat. Would you like some champagne?"

"Sure, that would be nice." And honestly I could take whatever social lubrication he was willing to provide me with. I was going to have to get into the right headspace for this to work at all.

He moved to uncork the bottle and it came off with a pop into the towel in his hands. Pouring us both a glass, he came around to sit beside me on the couch and handed me a glass.

"Here's to trying new things," he said with a grin.

"To new things," I said as we clinked glasses. I sipped the champagne slowly and enjoyed the taste of it on my tongue, trying to get my focus on something.

"Are you nervous, Samara?"

I shook my head. "No, I don't see any reason to be nervous."

"Are you sure?"

I nodded, but the truth was that my heart was going a mile a minute in my chest and there was a kind of thrill growing inside me. I wasn't nervous in a way that made me want to run and leave the penthouse—I almost wanted to grab Neil and kiss him right where we sat.

We sipped our champagne and he asked me questions about my life, what I enjoyed doing with my free time, and how I ended up at the club.

"My best friend, she had a job bartending there and told me they were looking for another bartender, so I jumped at the chance."

Neil nodded and looked me up and down again, his eyes slowly taking in my form. "Did you know what the club was when you first started working there?"

I laughed and that seemed to make him happy. "Well, it was difficult to miss after about the first time I walked in. There was a couple going at it in the pool like I was nothing. Then of course when I started serving I would often end up in some of the alcoves and private rooms, so I got a front row seat to a lot of things."

"And what did you think of that?" He asked as he traced a finger along the length of my forearm. It sent a shiver up my spine and made my breath catch in my throat.

"It was different...new...exciting." I could hardly latch on to a word, so distracted by his fingers tracing patterns on my skin.

He nodded and watched my face, taking in my different features. It was slightly unnerving to have him focusing so much intense attention on me.

"You're very beautiful, Samara. Do you realize how beautiful you are? That half of those men in the club see you walk by and want you? All the more because you are unattainable. They would give anything for you to be one of the ladies working the floor."

My lips had parted involuntarily and I was breathing a little heavier now. I was shocked at the effect Neil Vance was having on me, but not displeased. He had been so cocky, so demanding, but now in his presence I ached for something more from him.

As if reading my mind he leaned in and inhaled the scent of my perfume in the hollow of my neck. I quivered in anticipation, waiting for him to kiss or touch me in some way, but instead his lips hovered near my ear for a few silent, excruciating seconds.

Finally, he whispered: "I'm going to make you beg for it."

His hot breath sent a jolt down my spine and then he was on his feet again. "Follow me, dinner is waiting for us."

Neil led me over to the dining area of his penthouse, a corner completely surrounded by windows. The table was huge, big enough to seat 16 people easily, but tonight it was set for two at the very end. A cook brought out our plates and served us a light meal of salmon with herbed butter, fingerling potatoes, and thin green beans. Neil poured us more champagne and by the end of dinner and the second glass I was feeling the effect of the alcohol.

Our conversation was polite, not probing much into each other's personal lives. I think we must have both been unsure about what we were going to get into that night and I certainly had no idea what was in store for me.

"I know it seems a little early for bed, but we've got a lot to cover this week."

The statement took me off guard and created a lot of new questions in my mind.

"Come with me," he said, reaching out a hand.

I reached for him tentatively and let him lead me to his bedroom. It was nicely decorated and mostly in white. "We'll be here tonight, but other nights I may take you to another room. It seems important that this happens here, tonight."

I nodded, starting to understand what he was saying. This was the place it was going to happen. The place where he was going to rid me of my virginity and hopefully show me a little fun along the way. I had no doubt that the man was capable.

One entire wall of his bedroom was lined with windows. I looked at it warily and he noticed.

"Don't worry, I can control whether or not anyone can see inside here. So, whenever you feel like having an audience, you just let me know. But until then we'll keep this to ourselves."

"Thank you," I said with a smile. For the first time I saw something almost sweet in his face, but that glimmer disappeared almost as quickly as it had appeared.

"Take off your dress. I want to see you."

I could see how this was going to work. He told

me what to do. It made sense now, the dog collar. I reached around and unhooked the clasp at the top of the dress and drew the zipper down all the way until I could shrug out of the dress and let it fall to the floor.

I knew what I looked like, standing there in the bra and panties he had sent to me the day before. I knew that the sheer fabric of the lingerie hid absolutely nothing. I could feel my nipples harden under his gaze and as they puckered, feel them sticking out hard against the delicate lace.

"You're delicious, Samara. Thank you for wearing the lingerie. I've been dreaming of you in it for a while now. You'll be treated well for obeying my commands."

He moved over to a nightstand and pulled a stick with a feather tip out and brought it over to me. "How sensitive are you?" He asked as he lightly touched the feather to the skin of my arm and ran it all the way up to my shoulder.

"Very," I gasped. It was almost a tickle that I felt, but not quite. My breath was catching in tiny gasps and I could feel a shiver growing deep inside me. I wasn't cold, but I couldn't keep still.

He ran the tip of the feather back and forth across my breasts, drawing them into even harder peaks.

"You do like that," Neil said in what was almost a growl. "Now turn around, I want to see your ass."

I turned when I was told and he bent me over the bed. Expecting the feather again, I was surprised when he grabbed a handful of my ass and squeezed hard, bending over to whisper in my ear.

"You are mine tonight. Remember that. Remember that everything I do is for both of us. You are going to share in something with me that you have never known before."

Before I could even wonder what he meant, he drew his hand back and smacked me sharply on my right buttock, then immediately began rubbing it gently.

"I'll follow up every hard touch with a soft one, this much I promise you. You'll never feel any pain that isn't immediately followed by exquisite pleasure, but you are mine to use this week. And by the time we are done, you will be begging for me. You will do as I tell you, when I tell you, or you will be punished."

I didn't know what any of this really meant, but I had some idea. I was breathing heavily, thinking about the BDSM crowd that sometimes hung out around Club V. What would happen next? Whips? Would he tie me up?

He pulled me back up into a standing position. "There's something we've never done," he growled into my ear.

"There are lot of things we've never done," I responded without thinking.

He laughed and ran a finger down my cheek before cupping my face in his hands. "Samara, can I kiss you?"

I was surprised to hear him ask. Surprised that he didn't just claim my mouth right then without me granting permission. Not that it was necessary. In that moment, as I gazed into his deep blue eyes, I knew that Neil Vance could have whatever he wanted from me, whenever he wanted it.

I nodded consent and he pressed his lips to mine, gently at first and then it turned into a probing, passionate kiss and left me breathless and aching all the way down to my core.

When he pulled away there was a grin on his face. "You're delicious. And you know what else I know?"

I shook my head. It felt like this man could almost read my mind and I was afraid that he knew everything, all of it. That he could bend me over and take me there and then I would not complain.

"I know that you are horny as fuck, Samara. I can smell your wet pussy."

My knees had never gone weak from dirty talk before, but they did then and I gripped his biceps to steady myself.

"Are you?"

I took a deep breath. It was my time to be bold.

"Why don't you touch me and find out," I whispered.

Slowly he felt down the curve of my hip and put his hand between us, dipping his finger into my panties to stroke my silken folds. I sighed and closed my eyes as he did this, enjoying the sensation of him being there. My mind thought back to the first night I saw him, when that waitress had been in his office and he had done the same to her.

Now Neil Vance, one of the co-owner's of Club V was with me, his hands in my panties, and over the course of the next few hours he was going to be the one to take my virginity. I could hardly believe that any of it was real.

He removed his finger from between my pussy lips and brought it up to my mouth. "Taste yourself," he commanded. I opened my mouth and sucked his finger in, tasting my slick wetness on his digit. I sucked it clean and when he took it out of my mouth he leaned into kiss me again, diving deep with his tongue to get a taste of me.

"Mmm," he groaned when he pulled back.

"Taste me," I said, my eyes fierce and demanding.

I didn't have to suggest it twice. He had my panties down in a heartbeat and was on his knees, spreading my legs, kneeling to worship me. He flicked his tongue once and then twice against my clit and it sent a series of chills throughout my body. Then he leaned in to suck on it hard and insistent, sticking two of his fingers inside me. He thrust gently inside me and picked up the pace as I grabbed him by the hair and pressed him closer to me. I could feel myself losing control and the warmth of an intense orgasm building inside me.

"Please, please," I begged him. "Don't stop."

He didn't. I could tell he wouldn't dream of it, not

when I was that close. With a shudder I felt a small explosion inside me and a series of spasms of pleasure.

Neil leaned back and looked up at me. "You're so beautiful and I can't tell you how much I want you right now."

"You could," I said with a lazy giggle. My body was totally sated, but I knew I wanted more of him too. The question was whether or not he would let me have what I wanted. His dominance was clearly something that was very important to me and I didn't really know how it worked. He liked to please me, I had first hand evidence of that, but could I have what I wanted when I wanted it? Was I even allowed to ask?

"Can I ask you some questions, Neil? About how all of this works?"

"Certainly," he said as he scooped me up and placed me back on his bed. It was like a cloud and I sighed contentedly as I sank into the soft duvet.

"The collar, the dominance, what's it all about?"

"Ah, the collar. Well, I wondered if you would pick up on the clue in it. If you'll remember the first time we met, you saw Asia, who was wearing a collar similar to that one. I thought you might wonder if it was me."

I smiled as I pulled back the duvet and crawled underneath, urging Neil to follow me. He stripped down to his boxer briefs and slid between the sheets, pulling me close to him.

"Is this okay with you?" He asked. I didn't know why his asking was so surprising to me, but it made me glad that he wanted to check if things were fine with me before he proceeded.

"It feels nice," I said as I snuggled into the smooth expanse of his muscular chest. "Tell me more about the collar and things."

He took a deep breath, inhaling the scent of my shampoo. "You should know that while I sent it to you, I don't truly expect you to wear it. Wearing a collar is really a symbol of something and we're definitely not there yet. If you are interested in a submission relationship with me when this is all said and done, then I would be happy for us to discuss that. But I want to get to know you a little better. And there are a few things we need to take care of first."

I could feel his erection growing against my stomach and I reached up to trace the outline of his cock through the fabric of his underwear.

"Are you scared?" He asked.

I shook my head. "Not really. I'm looking forward to it. It's exciting."

His hand was between my legs again and he flicked at my still sensitive clit. With his other hand he unhooked my bra and I pulled it off, giving him full access to my breasts.

"These are incredible," he growled as he moved in to take one nipple into his mouth, sucking on it gently and then harder, until he had them both erect and sticking straight out from my breasts.

I was writhing underneath him and feeling somewhat neglectful that he wasn't getting as much attention so I reached down into his underwear to touch him and explore the silky length of his cock. He was already oozing precum and I wished I could get to him to lick it from the tip, but I could tell he had other plans.

"I want you, Samara. Now."

The intensity in his voice made me shudder and gasp. I spread my legs wider and let him move between them as he slid his boxer briefs off and tossed them aside. Then he quickly sheathed his cocked with a rubber.

"You're so wet. Samara, are you ready? I'll go slowly for you..." he leaned in closely to whisper into my ear, "but only this time."

I nodded furiously, the need in me growing by the second. "Please, I want you Neil."

I felt the tip of his cock probing at my tight entrance. Slowly, gently, he began pushing himself inside me. He was bigger than I realized and I felt myself getting accustomed to his size as he stretched me with every inch he pushed in. When he was finally buried inside me he let out a sigh and paused there for a moment.

"I hope this feels half as good to you as it does for me," he said, and I pulled him down to kiss me as he slowly began to withdraw and then thrust into me again. It was exquisite, this feeling of being filled and possessed. I could see why he leaned toward the dominance—because right now he owned me. He was claiming me as his own. And forever we would have this night, when I let him be the one to take my virginity.

His pace increased and I could tell by the look on his face that he was lost in the pleasure of it all. His eyes were half closed and his hips thrusted in and out of me, edging him closer to the moment of his climax.

I could feel something building as well. It was different with him inside me, and he was touching places I had never been touched before, not by fingers or a vibrator. It was as if he had access to a part of me that no one else had ever been able to reach. And every time he thrust himself into me it was a little closer to what felt like it was going to be a very intense orgasm.

With one final thrust punctuated by a groan, Neil let himself go and I felt him shudder inside me as I wrapped my legs around him and held him close, my own pleasure so overwhelming that I could do nothing but try to catch my breath.

He had bought and paid for me, and I was no longer a virgin.

# 9

How many more times had it been that night? I lost count after five. Neil had continued waking me up during the night, his hands roaming and exploring every inch of my body. I had never felt like this with anyone, ever. It was like he wanted to worship me and savor every second that we had together. I couldn't blame him for that. He was paying a high price to have me keep him company for the span of a week.

It felt natural waking up beside him the next morning, his arm casually thrown over the length of my body. He stroked the flesh of my hip as he woke and turned me over to face him.

"Good morning, Samara."

"Good morning, Neil," I said with a smile.

"Would you like some breakfast? I'll have Meredith whip up something for us if you like."

My stomach growled at the mention of breakfast.

"I'll take that as a 'yes' then." He picked up his phone, opened an app, and made a few selections before putting his phone aside again. "That just lets her know that I'm awake and to expect me in the kitchen in about 20 minutes."

"Why are you going to wait 20 minutes?"

"Because I have other plans," Neil said and he quickly made his other plans clear as he started to devour my body once again.

———

Breakfast was delicious, both that day and the next. Everything that Meredith cooked was exceptional and it seemed like less of a ridiculous expense to keep a cook and housekeeper on hand when she could put together meals like the ones I had been served.

On the second morning in the penthouse, after the first day was spent getting to know each other a little better and becoming accustomed to having the other person around, Neil said he had a surprise for me.

"What is it?" I asked as he led me down the hall.

"Remember how I said I had another bedroom?"

I nodded, wondering what kind of trap I might be walking into. It had been nonstop sex for the past 48 hours or so and I was starting to feel a little worn out.

"We're not..."

We stopped outside the bedroom door and he

pulled me close for a kiss. "We're not doing anything you don't want to do."

"But if you're the one in charge, you're the one telling me what to do, then how does it have anything to do with what I want?"

He grinned. "Think about it for a moment. Have I ever done anything you didn't want to do? Have I ever done anything with you that didn't bring you some form of pleasure?"

Neil was right, even though I hated to admit it. It was like he had unlocked the door to some secret part of me and set loose all of the secret desires I had. And somehow he had a good idea of what a lot of them were.

He opened the door and turned on the light. It was dim mood lighting, but I was still able to make out most of what filled the room. In the four corners there were different apparatuses. The things I recognized were a bondage bed and a bondage bench. All along the walls were different types of whips. In one corner there was a display of some very expertly tied rope. I had seen this sort of thing before and I wondered if Neil did the tying himself or if someone else did it. It had to be him. There was no way this guy was going to submit to anyone.

"Are you scared?" Neil asked. This was starting to seem like it was his favorite question.

"No." I said, completely honest about my feelings. "Some of this looks like it could be a lot of fun."

"I want you to take your clothes off. Now."

I gave him a sideways glance. "What if I don't want to?"

He inched ever closer to me and lowered his voice. "When have I ever told you to do something that didn't give you pleasure? Take off your clothes. I won't tell you again."

Rather than put up a fight, I stripped down to nothing and found the simple idea of standing here in this room with him, surrounded by all of his favorite toys, one of the most titillating experiences of my life. My nipples turned into small pebbles and I could feel my pussy contract in response.

"Kneel on the ground," he commanded.

I did as he said and he moved to the other side of the room where I couldn't see him. When he returned he had several feet of red rope for tying. He began with my arms, binding them in front of me wrapping the rope around and around itself. I had seen a performance like this before, but never dreamed that it would feel like this with the silkiness of the rope rubbing against my skin. More than that, it was the attitude and skill that Neil had about the act of tying me up.

My breathing became heavier as he wound the robe around me in an elaborate design. I lost all track of time, trying to focus on what he was doing, but getting lost in the movement of it, the way it felt as the rope began to tighten around my body.

Finally, when he was done, I was on the floor and completely bound, my heavy breasts jutting out in front of me obscenely. My nipples were painfully hard and I wanted to ask Neil to suck them, but I knew he would say no.

"You're going to stay there for a while and I'm going to look at you, my beautiful Samara."

A few minutes had passed when he stood next to me, placing an unseen object out of sight on the nearby nightstand. Neil ran his large hands down the length of me. I shivered with delight as his fingers drifted in tandem down across my breasts and my back, and then rose again, ever so gently to caress the length of me.

I could smell him, a heady mix of sex ... and musk.

One finger came to rest on my clit, as the other came to rest between my ass. Deftly, he slid his left hand down towards my asshole, pressing in suggestively as it went, until it came to rest on my now wet slit. This produced a deep laugh of amusement. "I see someone is happy." His voice was deep and sexy.

"Mmmm..." I gasped.

Neil's finger moved back and forth slightly, running the length of my slit, even as his other hand kneaded my clitoris. I shuddered beneath his touch, praying it would never stop.

This was something more, a deeper connection, a guilty delight of giving complete control to this man.

His fingers moved faster against my swollen clit.

I moved my hips to try and produce some friction against Neil's hand. His eyes were trained on me, when suddenly he pinched my clit hard. Jolts of pleasure and pain shot through my body, pulling out a rasping moan as I bucked from the sensation.

"You are a naughty little girl, aren't you?"

I could only nod in response.

Neil knelt down before my spread thighs. He looked up at me with a wicked grin that splayed across his face, "Ready for a little test?"

"Yes." I licked my lips, nervous now. What sort of test could this be? I was finding it hard to concentrate; I wanted Neil to touch me, to run his tongue across my wet slit, until I exploded with release.

Reaching up onto the bed beside me, Neil produced a large dildo, shaped to look like a man's penis. It had to be at least nine inches in length, and was quite thick. "I see you're already nice and wet, so we won't worry about any lubrication. Your test is to keep this in until I take it out. "

I'd never done something like this before. "What happens if I can't?"

"If you fail I will use the flogger – and not in a fun way." The amusement was gone from his eyes, replaced by a deadly seriousness.

I closed my eyes, nodding my approval to the challenge. How could I do otherwise?

Then, all at once, I could feel the head of the pseudo-cock pressing into me. My pussy was tight, and the sensation of this thick head pushing into me was intense, a heady combination of pleasure and pain as my walls stretched to accommodate.

Suddenly, just when I thought I'd tear in half, my body yielded, and the dildo plunged in, filling me. I'd felt so full, every inch of my pussy could feel the pseudo-skin of the shaft, replete with veins and ridges and bumps.

Frankly, it felt amazing.

Neil watched me intently, a small smile on his face. Clearly he understood exactly what I was feeling right now.

"Are you ready for your test?"

Ready for my test? What else could there be?

Seeing the puzzlement, Neil laughed, rocking back on his heels to climb off the bed. He leaned in and kissed me lightly on the lips, "Such an innocent. I'm going to have so much fun with you."

And then he was gone, striding to an table that held various gadgets. He began to look for something else. Out came a small remote and a long leather flogger.

My eyes widened in surprise; no, he couldn't really ...

Buried within me, the pseudo-cock began to pulse and vibrate.

The effect was instantaneous. Wetness flooded me as the vibrations hit every part of my pussy at once. Within seconds I was aching with need, so thoroughly aroused that it was hard to concentrate. My nipples were rock hard, eager to be suckled or tweaked or... anything, just something to provide a counterpoint to the wonders spreading outward from the dildo.

"This is the test," Neil smiled. "And to make it really hard, you're not going to be able to cum with the setting I've chosen."

"No!"

"Oh yes."

I writhed against the bed, my body on fire from the pulses within.

It became clear, however, that the vibrations from the dildo were too gentle to let me climax.

My eyes were trained on Neil now watching his every move as my body twitched as the vibrator pulsed within me. He walked to the door and turned to me, "I'll be back in a bit."

It felt like hours had gone by and my pussy ached from the strain of the dildo when I felt the buzzing finally stop. I was left in the room with only a halo that came from the small lighting in the corner. It didn't take long for sleep to take over. I was utterly spent and didn't care that I smelled of sex and still had the dildo inside of me.

---

NEIL CAME to me in the darkest hours of the night, sliding into the bed beside me where I lay sleeping, exhausted from the previous activities. The dildo had been removed and my bounds were now gone leaving my body aching.

His fingers moved in slow circles, to the bottom of my breasts, and then began to move south, in those same phantom patterns until I could feel the faintest trace atop my pussy.

I felt my nipples grow hard.

I opened my eyes, but couldn't see anything. No light came in from under the door, and the light had been turned off.

His fingers danced across my nipples, causing them to suddenly ache from the pleasure pain that the dildo had caused earlier. My body thrilled to his touch, wetness flooding me suddenly.

I realized that I was incredibly turned on by him, by the situation I now found myself in. A virgin only a few days ago and now I was lying in the dark with this man pressed against me, who was clearly going to fuck me until he was satisfied. It was exactly what I wanted, I realized.

I could feel my body responding, moving in time to his touch, my pussy beginning to ache.

He cupped my head with his right hand and tilted my face to the left so that he could kiss me. It was a deep passionate kiss, and it made my whole body tingle with pleasure. Yes, I was going to fuck him for all I was worth.

I smiled then, when I felt his thick, warm cock

press itself between my thighs. I lifted my left leg, allowing him to push his cock down in between my wet folds, moving easily amidst the wetness he found there.

Without waiting, Neil pushed into me, his girth filling me entirely. I shuddered and moaned out my pleasure. He felt amazing. I knew it was a cliché, but he just seemed to 'fit' me.

Shuddering with pleasure at the sudden sensation, I pushed back into him, craving more. He responded in kind, beginning to push into me and then withdraw ... slowly.

It was maddening, but every time I tried to push against him to increase my stimulation, he'd place his hand on my hip, stilling me, stilling himself too.

I whimpered each time he did this, needing him so much.

This went on for some time until finally he slid his right hand down to rest on my pussy. Deftly, he located my clit, and then began to knead it with his thumb and forefinger, using my own labia against me to stimulate me further.

I began to gasp, my breath coming in short heaves as I tried to retain some degree of control over my body.

It was useless, I realized. He simply knew exactly what to do, knew what I needed; knew how to take me to the ragged edge of my orgasm and then leave me at that edge, pausing to let me calm herself, only to resume again without warning so that I was surprised by my own pleasure each time.

Jesus Christ!

My mind raced, trying to stay ahead of the delirious sensations of his finger drifting over my skin. My pussy throbbed as he continued moving in and out of me, the fullness of his cock filling me and then receding with maddening slowness.

He was making love to me, I realized, taking his time to pace himself and immerse me in my own pleasure. I shuddered as he pushed into me again, gradually filling me completely with his thick cock.

I was so wet, and yet our embrace remained utterly silent. Not like the dirty, noisy sex I'd expected. No, he was utterly silent, just the sound of his breathing in my ear. The warmth and the touch of it against my ear and my neck added to the overall stimulation of his fingers, one of which was caressing my full right breast, while his left hand kept its firm friction on my aching clit.

In ... and out again...and then in slowly...lingering, just for a moment while my clit throbbed and pulsed beneath his touch...and then pulling out, his cock filling me even as it withdrew...until I was devoid of him, feeling empty from his absence...yet gasping from the pleasure that was flooding through me from my breasts ... and then mewling out in joy as that marvelous cock pressed again into me, one long, slow, smooth motion ... his shape melding into mine ... the contours of his cock seeming to fit naturally against the sensitive pleasurable spots within me.

My god it felt like heaven and I completely abandoned myself to the pleasure.

I could feel the wave coming, knew that my body was building and surging towards an orgasm.

It felt wicked, sinful, to let this man take my body the way that he had for the last several days.

But now, in this bed, covered in the sweat of my own passion, the smell of my own sex thick in my nostrils as my pussy grasped again and again at this magnificent cock that filled me, I didn't care.

I only wanted to be fucked. To drown myself in that sensation of being filled by that pulsing cock; to feel my body move in time against Neil regardless of whatever shreds of willpower I had left.

Determined to gain some small measure of control, I ground my rear into his groin – and smiled as he moved in time against me, his thick cock pressing into me, parting the shivering lips of my sopping pussy.

I smiled to myself in the darkness, suddenly happy beyond words, savoring the moment. And finally, in the darkness, I surrendered all resistance, and let go.

It had been at least an hour, an hour of his hands on my body, playing my most sensitive areas like an instrument. An hour of his thick cock within me, driving me onward to pleasure.

I could feel his cock throb suddenly and then spasm, pulsing with life and pleasure as he let go. And then, just as he came, my body bucked and writhed against his as I exploded into an orgasm. Stars errupted in front of my eyes in the darkness as I let out a long, loud shuddering cry.

At last I collapsed in his arms, my breasts heaving in time with my hurried gasps. Neil nuzzled into me, holding me tight; I felt loved and secure and glorified as a woman all at the same time.

---

IT WAS ONLY THE BEGINNING. Leather, feathers, whips, gags…I felt like he tried it all on me, and strangely—at least strangely to my mind in those moments—I loved every bit of it. I loved it when he blindfolded me and teased every area of my body. I was frustrated, but ultimately pleased the most whenever he left me tied to the bed for a few hours after he had edged me closer and closer to orgasm several times, but never let me have release. When he finally came back to me that time, hours later, I was still begging him to fuck me. And this time he did, harder and deeper than he had before. It was the most intense orgasm I had experienced, but he wouldn't let me stop there. No, he wasn't done and he commanded me to keep coming until he was ready. I didn't know it was possible, for my body to be wracked so hard with pleasure, but he showed it to me again and again as the days went on. Just when I thought I had experienced the ultimate, he brought me to a new height. And I wondered how on earth I would ever leave this man. He had brought so much to me and taught me so much in so little time. I knew then that, eventually, I would wear the collar. I was his Samara.

## 10

Saturday came around all too soon. After a week of fun together, it was coming to an end. Neil had decided to come into the bathroom and watch me bathe after we made love for several hours that morning, waking long before sunrise and ending up on the floor, in front of the massive windows in his bedroom, early morning sunlight streaming down on our naked bodies.

He sat by the tubs edge and watched me as I finished cleaning up. "All done," I chimed cheerfully.

Neil held out a towel for me and helped me out of the massive tub. He wrapped the big fluffy towel around my body and began drying me off. It was a kind of treatment I still wasn't used to, but knew that I could learn to love very quickly. It was so much fun to have someone showing me this kind of attention almost 24 hours each day. But I still had some questions in my mind. I knew he felt very strongly about me, but was this the kind of relationship that he wanted to make exclusive? We hadn't talked about it and if I was going to be true to my feelings, I thought it was a little early to commit to too much. I was open to hearing what Neil wanted out of this, but I was also fine with keeping my options open. Just because we had slept together didn't mean that I needed to give everything up and jump right into a relationship with this guy.

We were both quiet as he dried me off. Then as I was standing there naked, he turned me around to face him and planted a kiss on my lips.

"Last day. How do you feel about it?"

I looked around the opulent bathroom. "You've gotten me used to a standard of living I won't be able to sustain outside of this palace of a penthouse you live in."

Neil laughed. "I'll see if I can talk to your manager about a raise."

I looked at him cautiously. "You wouldn't, would you?"

"If you wanted me to, I could. Definitely."

I shook my head slowly and firmly. "I don't want anything that has happened here between you and I to have an effect on the way things are for me at work. It would be too much for me to deal with. I might not have known who you were to start with, but I am sure there are plenty of other people I work with who know exactly who you are. Having them know that we had any kind of association...it would..."

"It would make things difficult for you. I understand." Neil reached for my clean clothes and handed them over to let me get dressed.

Once I had some clothing on I turned to face him again.

"What do you expect once you get back to normal life?"

I thought for a moment. What did I expect?

"I think I'll be focusing on my brother and my parents for the foreseeable future. You?"

Neil was quiet as he looked in the mirror. "I think I need to spend more time with my parents. We're close, but life has a way of...getting in the way I guess. They've always been such great role models for me and I would like to be around them more, soak up some of their wisdom. Figure out how they managed to find their soulmates so young and stay married for 40 years."

"Forty years? Wow. I thought my parents had been together for a while. I guess compared to most people they have, but yours..."

Neil nodded. "It's really something. I know that the line of work I have chosen and the sorts of recreation I enjoy may not make this easy to believe, but I've always wanted that." He turned to look at me then. "To get married and have kids, have a real family of my own. I know I'm not ancient by any means, but I'm 31 and it seems like it's time to start getting serious about all of this."

I nodded in agreement, still not quite sure what to say about that. "I guess we'll both have some family obligations to get back to."

Neil tilted his head uncertainly. "Mine is more about spending time, yours...well, you've got some real obligations in front of you. Josh will need you now more than ever."

I'm not sure if I would have noticed exactly what he said if he had left the long, lingering pause there at the end of his statement.

"I never told you my brother's name was Josh. Did Elle tell you? Someone else at the club?"

He could have found his way out right then, but instead he shook his head and said the last thing I expected to hear.

"Samara, I know Josh. In fact, I've known your brother for some time now."

## 11

"How do you know Josh?" I asked, completely baffled as to what connection Neil Vance, owner of Club V, could have with my brother.

"Come on, let's go to the roof. Meredith will bring up breakfast. I'll tell you all about it."

Neil grabbed a blanket and we went upstairs to the roof terrace and sat on one of his outdoor sofas. The morning was bright, but it was chilly and the blanket had been a great idea.

I curled up close to him and rested my head on his shoulder. "So, tell me."

He took a deep breath as he stroked my hair gently. "I don't want you to get freaked out about it when I tell you the whole reason I first met your brother. See, after that first night that I met you, I couldn't get you out of my head. Sure, I could have shown up at the club to see you, talk to you, maybe ask you out, but I had a really good idea that you would turn me down if I did that."

I laughed. "Your instincts were right there."

"So give me a little credit as far as that is concerned. I looked into who you were, where you were from, your background and all of that, but the thing that caught my eye was that you had a younger brother who went to the school where my brother coaches."

I sat straight up. "Your brother...is Coach Vance?" I had heard Josh talk about the guy several times and he had been one of the people who came to see Josh most often in the hospital over the past couple of weeks. "I had no idea, I mean, I never would have made the connection there."

Neil shrugged. "Of course not, there was no need to. Anyway, it just so happens that I sometimes go down to Jersey to help my brother out with practices. There have been a few times that he's had to miss practice because of some kind of family thing with his kids and I've filled in for him when he's needed me. So actually I had met your younger brother before I ever met you, I just didn't realize it until later."

I couldn't stop staring at him now. "What a strange world it can turn out to be sometimes, the fact that you had already met my brother when we were working in a setting where we could have run into each other at any time."

"I know, it's crazy," Neil agreed as he planted a kiss on my forehead.

"Okay, so wait though. When did you find out about his transplant surgery? Was it when you saw my application for the auction come through?"

He shook his head, but was quiet for a moment as Meredith came up with a tray full of breakfast items.

"Thank you," I said as she set them all on the coffee table in front of us. I was hungry, as I had been all week with the increased activity, but I was more interested in hearing the rest of Neil's story.

When Meredith had gone he spoke again. "It was a little while after he collapsed at the football game. My mom had told me that there had been some kind of accident at the game or something, but it wasn't until about a week later that I got the real details from Brad. We had a charity event that my family often donates to and Brad and I were there, as each other's date I guess you could say, because my parents were double booked that night and couldn't make it for the event. I didn't mind, it was always a good place to make some connections and hand out business cards. You never know who might be the next club member."

"Anyway, Brad told me what had happened with Josh and I...honestly I had to keep myself from calling you that night, asking what your family needed, and rushing over. I hated the thought that all of you were in pain or that you were struggling to figure out how you were going to pay for such a drastic surgery. I knew what an ordeal that was going to be to pay for something like that because I remember when I was a kid and my mom had cancer. It was a struggle for us then. Having a family member who is sick and could potentially die has got to be one of the most difficult things anyone can go through."

He brushed a bit of my hair out of my face and turned my chin toward him. "Are you doing okay in there? I mean, really?"

I nodded and offered him the tiniest of smiles. "Really, most days I am fine. Mostly I worry about my mom and how she is coping with the stress of it all. I know how my dad copes and I can tell by the number of absolutely gutted cars parked out back of his garage right now that he is getting any of that excess energy and grief out of his body and into something productive."

"But you," he said. "What about you, Samara?"

I inhaled deeply, smelling the coffee wafting up from the tray.

"I worry that I am going to lose him. I worry that none of this will work out or that the surgery will be a failure and we will lose my brother right there on the table. It is absolutely my worst nightmare, Neil. The boy is just a kid. I know he's only a couple of years younger than me, but I am his big sister and I will forever be that. All I want to do is protect him and tell him that everything is going to be okay. For the first time in my life I can't do that for him. There is nothing that me or my mom or my dad can do to make his fears go away. And it feels fucking unfair."

I was sobbing now and I couldn't remember when it started, but Neil pulled me into an embrace and held me close while I cried.

"And so you did what you knew you were able to do. You decided to give up a part of yourself so that you could do your part in saving your brother. It's really admirable, Samara. I don't think it's something that everyone would do."

I looked up at him and wiped the tears from my eyes. "You know what though? The thing that surprises me most about all of this is that I don't feel like I gave anything up."

"What do you mean?" Neil asked.

"I mean that my whole life I have been told that my virginity was some kind of big deal, and in the end it really wasn't. Not that it wasn't a 'big deal', you are a very big deal, Neil." We both laughed at this. "But what I mean is that I don't feel like I gave anything away. I didn't lose any part of me. I simply opened up a door to a new part. There are things I can experience now that I never had before."

"I should think you've already experienced a few new things so far this week."

I grinned. "You have shown me a new universe to explore. I don't know where I would be without you, honestly."

Neil poured us each a cup of coffee and we sat

enjoying the warm brew in the cool, crisp, spring morning air. It was beautiful up there, above the city, where everything had a kind of pinky golden glow to it in the first light of the morning.

"While we're being honest, there's probably something I should tell you," Neil said with some hesitation.

"What's that?"

"First of all, let me just say that I never intended to keep something from you, but I wasn't sure you would ever see me otherwise. I could tell the sort of opinion you had of me the first time we met and I knew that I didn't stand a chance. Even getting to know your brother, there was never going to be an opportunity for me to use that to my advantage and get you to go out on a date with me. And rumors run rampant at the club. The minute you had mentioned me to Suzy she would have been able to tell you twelve different things about me. Seriously, how did you never hear any of those things in the length of time that you worked there?"

I shrugged and took another sip of my coffee. "I don't listen to gossip." I said matter-of-factly.

Neil rolled his eyes. "Well, I'm glad you're able to avoid it. Anyway, I knew you weren't going to see me. I knew my chances sucked. So when I saw your name pop up in the stack of names that was going to go out to our elite members, I grabbed it before it could go anywhere. You literally never left my office once your name entered the building. Of course Elle already knew because she had compiled the list, but I told her to remove you from it immediately and that I was going to pay whatever the asking price was. I felt like some kind of crazed, lovesick guy in a stupid rom-com, doing whatever I could to make sure no one else could get their hands on you."

He squeezed me tightly then and buried his nose in my hair, breathing me in.

"We are careful about who we let in, but when I think about who could have had their hands on you...it makes me sick. And how close it all came to happening. But I got to you in time."

I was struggling to understand what the thing was that he was trying to be honest about. "I already knew that you basically called dibs on me early on. Elle explained to me how that works."

"Yes, but there is something else that Elle didn't know about all of this."

"What's that?" I asked, truly confused at this point.

Neil looked me straight in the eyes. "Samara, I was going to pay for your brother's surgery anyway. I had it on my agenda that day to make the call to Brad to find out who I needed to speak to about paying the medical bill. I had already written the blank check out to your parents, but then I saw your name."

He paused to look at me, measuring my response. I was surprised by his admission, but not shocked. So he had always been willing to pay, that wasn't a question. What he was admitting was that he had used the situation to his own advantage, to get to me and get what he wanted.

I reached up and touched his cheek gently. "Neil, I can hardly blame you. I had no way of knowing that you were going to do that for my brother. But it's so kind of you. I think it shows the kind of heart you really have."

He grasped my hand and pulled it to his chest. "The kind of heart I have is the kind that would do anything to get close to you. I would have paid anything to have this week with you. The fact that it could have ever been reality was more than I could have dreamed of."

I leaned in and kissed him gently on the lips.

"Last day," I said.

"Indeed," he nodded. "Are you ready for me to take you home?"

I looked out across the expanse of the cityscape and shook my head. It was too beautiful to leave here just yet.

"You know, I think I can stay a little longer."

# EPILOGUE

Six Months Later

I palmed the back of my neck nervously and then turned to look up at Neil. He smiled, looking down at me, indicating everything was going to be just fine. It had been a long road for my brother. The transplant had gone well although they had kept him in the hospital a little longer than expected as a precaution.

I could feel the sweat in my palms as I stood hand in hand with Neil on my parents front porch. Everyone had been invited to celebrate Josh's return home. He had been released from the hospital a month prior but my mom felt it would be better to wait rather than to have so much anxiety and commotion so soon afterwards.

Neil and I had been inseparable since our first week together. We were two people that molded together like a puzzle. We were each other's soulmate. People always say one is lucky to find their soulmate and that sometimes it doesn't happen at all, so I guess we could both count our lucky stars that we found one another. After spending so much time with Neil, I quickly learned that he had the same interests and goals in life as me. He was a true family man at heart and when I had the chance to meet his folks two months ago it made me fall in love with him all that much more.

The kicker was when we had dinner with his folks one evening. We were all about to dive into the wonderful meal his mother had just cooked for us when Neil stood with his glass of champagne in his hand.

"Mom, Dad, I have an announcement to make." He said, looking at both of them and then he turned to me and smiled. His eyes sparkling with a happiness that I had come to enjoy seeing. "Honey, you are the love of my life." Neil paused and sat his glass on the table as he got down on one knee and reached into his pocket. I watched in shock as he pulled out a burgundy velvet box. Neil looked up at me then and smiled, "I know we have only been together six months, but you, Samara are everything I have ever dreamed of. You make me complete in every way. Would you do the honor of becoming my wife?" Neil asked as he opened the box revealing a five carat yellow canary princess cut engagement ring.

In one fluid motion my hand flew to my mouth. I was in shock and had absolutely no idea that he was going to propose. I could feel the tears pool in my eyes and then spill over onto my cheeks. I smiled and finally whispered, "Yes! Yes! I would love to be your wife!" I couldn't stop my hand from shaking as he slid the large engagement ring onto my finger. I was mesmerized and then finally snapped out of my reverie and threw my arms around his neck. A moment later his parents started clapping and we turned to them to see their smiles.

"Oh honey. We're so happy for you." His mother said, getting up and giving us both a hug and his father followed suit right after.

So now I stood here on my parents porch with the love of my life, nervous as hell as to how everyone will react to the news. A moment later I opened the door and walked in to see my parent's small living room busy with friends and family chatting among themselves.

"Honey, you made it." My mom said, rushing over to greet us.

"Of course, Mom. I wouldn't miss it for the world." I kissed her gently on the cheek and then motioned to Neil. "Mom, you remember Neil?"

"Yes, of course. It's so nice to see you again." She said, pulling him in for a hug. My mom was never one for hand shaking. "Come in and say 'Hi' to everyone. I'll let your brother know you're here."

We made our way into the room and my rounds of hello's and hugs to everyone while introducing Neil to the folks he hadn't met yet, when finally Josh walked in from the kitchen. A grin from ear to ear splayed on his face. God, it was so good to see him feeling stronger; his old self.

"Hey you." I said smiling and pulling him into a hug. "How you feeling?" I asked looking up him.

"I feel good. Getting stronger every day." Josh smiled. "Hey Neil. So glad you came, man. Your brother's in the kitchen raiding all the food."

Neil laughed and gave Josh a light pat on the shoulder. "Glad you're feeling better buddy."

After an hour went by, my mom and dad brought out a celebration cake for Josh and we watched as he blew out the candles and thanked everyone for coming. I sat next to Neil on the love seat as my mom and dad made a quick speech about family, the unknown and to never take anything for granted in life. As they held their glasses up to say cheers to everyone, we did as well. I took a sip of my wine and then felt Neil release my hand and stand. My heart began to beat wildly when he started to speak.

"Mr. & Mrs. Tanza, everyone. I also have something I would like to share with you all." He said and then looked down at me. He reached for my hand and pulled me to my feet to stand beside him. When I looked up at the crowd, my eyes instantly fell on my mother and then to my dad. She could always read me like a book. She was holding her hand over her mouth almost ready to cry and my dad had a wide grin on his face.

"I would like to announce that I proposed to Samara a little time ago and she accepted. We're getting married!" He said cheerfully.

I caught my brother's eye and he gave me a proud smile and a thumbs up.

As the crowd broke out in a cheer I watched my parents walk to us. "Congratulations honey. We are so happy for you both." They said, giving us each a kiss and hug.

"You knew?" I asked looking at my dad.

"Of course. You don't go ahead with something like without asking the parents permission first now do you?" He said giving Neil a quick wink.

"Honey, I didn't want to freak you out. A week before I proposed, I met your parents for lunch. I didn't feel comfortable proposing until I asked for their blessing first. I hope you're not upset?"

I smiled to myself feeling a little foolish about being so nervous. I should have known he would have done this. Neil was an old fashioned soul. I gave him a slap on the arm and said, "It's okay. You have the rest of your life to make it up to me."

***Club V series continues with* Undone!**

Taylor Dawson spends her days getting down and dirty as a mechanic at her father's garage, rather than with a hot guy. At nineteen, she's so ready to get rid of her 'v' card but hasn't found the right man yet. Collecting her roommate from her bartending job at Club V, Taylor stumbles across Club Owner, Jake Mesa, giving a lesson in submission. Tay doesn't think she'd ever be able to obey like the collared woman at Jake's mercy and slips away from the room unnoticed.

However, Jake's security footage caught the gorgeous voyeur in his room and now she has his full attention. When Taylor's dad admits to a business disaster that could end not only the garage but his life, she doesn't know where to turn. Then Jake makes her an offer...
Will she be able to resist or become completely undone?

**Read Undone now!**

## GET A FREE BOOK!

Join my mailing list to be the first to know of new releases, free books, special prices and other author giveaways.

http://freehotcontemporary.com

## ALSO BY JESSA JAMES

### Bad Boy Billionaires

Lip Service

Rock Me

Lumber Jacked

Baby Daddy

Billionaire Box Set 1-4

### The Virgin Pact

The Teacher and the Virgin

His Virgin Nanny

His Dirty Virgin

### Club V

Unravel

Undone

Uncover

### Cowboy Romance

How To Love A Cowboy

How To Hold A Cowboy

Beg Me

Valentine Ever After

Covet/Crave

Kiss Me Again

Handy

Bad Behavior

Bad Reputation

Dr. Hottie

# ABOUT THE AUTHOR

Jessa James grew up on the East Coast but always suffered a severe case of wanderlust. She's lived in six states, had a variety of jobs and always comes back to her first true love – writing. Jessa works full time as a writer, eats too much dark chocolate, has an iced-coffee and Cheetos addiction, and can't get enough of sexy alpha males who know exactly what they want – and aren't afraid to say it. Dominant, alpha-male insta-luv is her favorite to read (and write).

Sign up HERE for Jessa's Newsletter:

http://jessajamesauthor.com/mailing-list/

Follow me on BookBub:

www.ingramcontent.com/pod-product-compliance
Lightning Source LLC
LaVergne TN
LVHW011836060526
838200LV00053B/4060